noted Ironton status 20

20/1002

MW01181581

WITHDRAWN

03-1898

F   Horton, Robert J.
HOR   The hanging X.

$25.95

THE HANGING X

THE HANGING X

A Western Story

ROBERT J. HORTON

Five Star • Waterville, Maine

First Edition
First Printing: August 2003

Published in 2003 in conjunction with
Golden West Literary Agency.

Set in 11 pt. Plantin by Minnie B. Raven.

Printed in the United States on permanent paper.

Library of Congress Cataloging-in-Publication Data

Horton, Robert J., d. 1934.
    The hanging X : a western story / by Robert J. Horton.
    p. cm.
    ISBN 0-7862-3780-5 (hc : alk. paper)
    I. Title.
PS3515.O745H67 2003
    813'.52—dc21   2003044882

THE HANGING X

Foreword

by

Jon Tuska

When Robert J. Horton died in a hotel room in Manhattan from bronchial pneumonia probably complicated by chronic myocarditis from which he had suffered for years, he was forty-four years old. The date of his death was January 19, 1934. Samuel C. Glasgow, M.D., had been his personal physician since August, 1927, and he was attending him when he died. At the time Horton was widowed, and he had maintained his residence in New York City for twenty-one years, although he spent much of his time away from the city, traveling. Since 1920 he had made his living writing Western fiction for the magazine market, primarily after 1922 for Street & Smith. By the mid 'Twenties Horton was one of three authors to whom Street & Smith paid 5¢ a word—the other two being Frederick Faust, perhaps better known as Max Brand®, and Robert Ormond Case. Many of Horton's serials for Street & Smith's *Western Story Magazine* were subsequently brought out as books by Chelsea House, Street & Smith's book publishing company. Although virtually all of Horton's stories appeared under his byline in the magazine, for their book editions Chelsea House published them either as by Robert J. Horton or by James Roberts. Sometimes, as was the case with *Rovin' Redden* (Chelsea House, 1925) by James Rob-

7

erts, a book would consist of three short novels that were editorially joined to form a "novel". Other times the stories were serials published in book form, such as *Whispering Cañon* (Chelsea House, 1925) by James Roberts or *The Man of the Desert* (Chelsea House, 1925) by Robert J. Horton. It may be obvious that Chelsea House, doing a number of books a year by the same author, thought it a prudent marketing strategy to give the author more than one name. The same practice was followed with Faust's novels that appeared variously from Chelsea House as by George Owen Baxter or by David Manning. Max Brand® was the named reserved for Faust novels published by Dodd, Mead.

Despite the fact that Horton claimed New York City residence for so many years, in 1923 he was living in an apartment in Santa Barbara; in 1924 he was in Los Angeles for part of the year and for the rest of it in London, England. Horton had been born in Coudersport, Pennsylvania, of an American father and a Colombian mother, and occasionally he would also return to Coudersport for periods of time, as he did in December, 1924, and into 1925, before living for a time in Highlands, New Jersey. Later in 1925 his mailing address was in Paris, France. He apparently liked the state of Maine since he would spend long periods there as well, at Oquossoc, Rumford, Rangleley, and Portland.

In the years 1920 through 1922, Horton published a total of fifteen Western stories in *Adventure Magazine*. It was doubtless one of these stories that Walt Coburn was reading, as he recalled in his autobiography, *Walt Coburn: Western Word Wrangler* (Northland Press, 1973). "There were enough mistakes to convince me the writer did not savvy anything about cowpunching," Coburn wrote. "It was only after I had finished the yarn, which had enough plot and character delineation to make good reading in spite of my biased opinion, that I looked to find the name of the author. The story was written by Robert J. Horton, and this surely rang a bell. The author was the same old friend and drinking companion I had known back in Great Falls, Montana. The same Bob Horton who was sports editor for the *Great Falls Tribune*, with a daily column under the byline of 'Sporticus'. I had been completely out of touch with Bob for a number of years, and had no idea he had started writing Western fiction."

Coburn wrote a long letter to Horton, in care of *Adventure*, telling Horton that his cowpunching days were over and that now he wanted to write Western fiction. The tutelage Horton provided Coburn proved invaluable, and it was not long before Coburn himself was having his name showcased on the covers of Western fiction magazines, including Horton's own staple market, *Western Story Magazine*.

However much time Horton may have spent living in the American West prior to 1922, he rarely went there at all after that time. His Western stories are concerned most of all with character, and it is the characters that drive the plots rather than the other way around. It is unfortunate he died at such a relatively early age. Many of his novels, after Street & Smith abandoned Chelsea House, were published only in British editions, and Robert J. Horton was never to appear at all in paperback books. I imagine his name has been generally forgotten, as was also the case with Cherry Wilson. *The Hanging X* was a book-length novel that appeared in the American market only in a condensed version. It was written during late September and October of 1932 at Saranac Lake, New York, and Horton titled it "Stepson of the Hanging X". Street & Smith changed the title to

"The Hanging X" when it appeared in *Western Story Magazine* in the issue dated February 25, 1933. It was still the time of the Great Depression, and Horton, as all the other Street & Smith writers including Frederick Faust, had been told he would have to accept less for his stories. In this case he was paid only 2¢ a word and his story was abridged so that it could appear in a single issue of the magazine rather than as a serial which had been the author's intention in writing it.

Portland, Oregon
October, 2002

Chapter One

The whole of the north range from the Teton to the line stood aghast, still stunned and vaguely wondering, although it was nearly a week since the double tragedy. Nate Martin, powerful overlord and owner of the great Hanging X Ranch, and his wife, Sally Landon Martin, had both lost their lives on the same day in an accident such as none on that vast range would have believed could have happened to Nate—in a runaway.

It was early in May and the prairie remained soggy in spots, with coulées running water and the Teton River at flood. There had been heavy snows with the calendar advent of spring, followed by a warm Chinook wind and a warmer sun that had started the snow melting earlier in the mountains than usual and had distended the creeks into swollen torrents. The cattle, weakened by the severity of the winter, had been caught in the bogs, where they had died by scores, unable to extricate themselves. The grass had turned green overnight, killing more cows and steers as they fed greedily upon it. It was an early season of disaster.

Nate had ordered two spanking bays, just in from winter pasture, hitched to a single buckboard and had driven with his wife along the river road before the bottoms to show her the havoc that had been wrought. None knew what had frightened the horses to cause them to bolt up a grade close to a cutbank, veer sharply, and overturn the buckboard, spilling Nate and the woman over the bank.

The stockman had been caught in some driftwood in the river and drowned. His wife had plunged on some rocks, breaking her frail body. Two ranch hands who had chanced to see the accident had taken Mrs. Martin to the ranch house, sounded the alarm, and later recovered Martin's body. A doctor reached the ranch just before midnight, too late to do anything for the dying woman. He had heard her mutter the name of her own son, Gail Landon, who was Nate Martin's stepson.

After the numbing horror had worn away, those who had heard the news asked themselves who would fall heir to the thousands of acres of deeded lands, the thousands of additional acres of range, the great herds and other property that comprised the Hanging X. Mostly they were disturbed by the thought of Gail, Sally Martin's son by a first marriage. For Nate had married but once—his choice being the widow of Jim Landon, a former railroad man—and he had no children of his own. None, not even Martin or his wife, would acknowledge having seen Gail in almost five years.

On this sunny afternoon, five days after the fatal accident, three men were sitting in the large living room of the ranch house. Two of the men, Sheriff Will Woods and Henry Compton, banker, had long known Nate Martin. The third, Frank P. Griffin, was an attorney who Nate had consulted occasionally on legal affairs. All three were from the town of Riverhead, the county seat.

The lawyer was a man of forty-odd years, tall with proportionate breadth of shoulders and weight, with alert brown eyes. He had been practicing in the county for fifteen years and had a reputation for being shrewd and able, and well read in the law. He sat at a table in the center of the comfortable room, holding some legal-appearing papers in his hands, eyeing Sheriff Woods and Henry Compton who sat across from him. He put down the papers, leaned back in his chair, and spoke rapidly and concisely.

"There seems to be no question of the veracity of the report I have from the doctor," he said. "When he arrived here before midnight the day of the accident, he found Nate Martin dead. He had been drowned. His wife was still living and recovered consciousness for a brief interval before she died. The doctor had witnesses. So it is clearly established that Martin died first."

The sheriff and the banker looked at each other, nodded, and said nothing.

"That fact is important," Griffin continued. "You heard me read the wills. Nate Martin left everything to his wife save for minor bequests to a few employees. Missus Martin, then, owned the great bulk of the estate at the time of her death." He paused as if to let this sink into the minds of the other two men.

"There ain't any question about that," said Compton, "and he made no provision to be observed in case of her death before or after his own."

"Precisely," Griffin agreed. "Now, in her will, as you've heard, she leaves everything to her son, by her first marriage, Gail Landon. Nate Martin, as I knew him and as I've heard many times, was always a taciturn man in regard to his personal affairs. He never mentioned having any other relatives. He came to this part of the country as a youth, fought for what he got, and married rather late in life. Isn't that so, Sheriff?"

"He was a first settler, you might say," Woods drawled, "like myself, although he was here ahead of me. I never heard him speak of any relatives."

"There seems to be small possibility of anyone ever

turning up to contest his will, if that's what you're getting at," said the banker.

"I was getting at that," Griffin affirmed, "and now it is disposed of. With the exception of the few bequests Martin made, his estate went to his wife when he died. When Sally Martin died later, it went to her own son, Gail Landon. I drew both wills. Therefore, Gail Landon is the heir and we've got to find him." He looked straight at the sheriff.

"I suppose that'll be my job," said Woods with a frown. "You say nothing was found in the papers you've looked over here that would show where Gail is now?"

"Nothing," the lawyer replied. "If his mother received letters from him, she destroyed them, possibly fearing that Nate would run across them. We all know that Nate had no use for him."

"That's right," said the banker. "Why should he? The boy was man-size when he was sixteen and wilder than he had any business to be. It was scrape after scrape, and finally guns. He was nineteen when Nate gave him a thousand dollars and kicked him off the ranch. He's nearly twenty-four now, and, if he's kept on going like he started, he's liable to be dead, or in jail, or . . . worse."

"He had plenty of spirit," the sheriff admitted.

"That's something that we have nothing to do with now," said Griffin firmly. "He was pretty woolly and wild, all right, with the making of a deadly gunman in him. Every time I talked with him, I could see the lust for adventure shining in his eyes. Personally I think Nate was prejudiced against him from the start because he was a stepson. He may have sown his wild oats by now and straightened out. We've got to give him the benefit of the doubt because we must face the fact that he is now the owner of the Hanging X, which you'll agree is a considerable responsibility."

14

"That's just what I'm afraid of," Compton blurted. "It'll be too much for him. And he's of age so we can't appoint a guardian."

"I reckon we'd better hold our tongues till we see him an' have a talk with him," Woods drawled, his mild blue eyes lighted with a tolerant glow.

"Yes, Compton." Griffin smiled. "The sheriff is right, and you may have to make Gail a director in your bank to take the place of his stepfather."

The banker started, and then stared as if this hadn't occurred to him.

"We may all have to cater a little to him," said Woods dryly.

"The first thing," Griffin resumed, "is to get word to him. As you hinted, Sheriff, this is right in your department."

"Yes, get him here, or in Riverhead, first," growled the banker. "You ought to be able to find out where he is with your connections."

"I was able to keep track of him till he left the state," said the sheriff. "After that I wasn't so much interested. I always figured he'd turn up someday an' let it go at that. I think we better have that foreman, Stagg, in here again. He used to think Gail's tricks were smart an' always showed an interest in him. It might just be that he has an idea where Gail is, although I don't know where he'd get it."

"Stagg's sore because Nate didn't leave him more," Compton observed, frowning again. "He's another one. I don't see why Nate should have left him anything."

Sheriff Woods tugged at his gray mustache. "He's been here a long time," he said. "He was a valuable man when rustlin' still was in style around these parts."

"If he knows where Landon is, it's a wonder he didn't

try to get in touch with him before the funeral," said Griffin. "Maybe he did for that matter. You better call him, Sheriff."

Woods rose and looked from one to the other of them. "Be careful how you talk when Stagg's here," he said. "He's touchy."

He went out the open front door to the porch and they heard him calling to someone in the courtyard. "See if Stagg's in the bunkhouse, or around, an' send him here," came his voice.

Presently he returned and resumed his seat as footsteps and the jingle of spurs came from the end of the porch. A moment later Stagg, the ranch foreman, entered the room, his hat in his hand.

A different atmosphere seemed to fill the room as the man stood there at the end of the table nearest the door, towering before them. He was not as large a man as the attorney, but he gave more of an impression of physical strength. His eyes were set far apart and were brittle with the keen, darting lights in them. A full nose above rather thin lips, straight and tight, gave him an aggressive appearance. His face was tanned and seamed. His holster was empty at the moment, and the absence of a gun seemed out of keeping with his rough dress. He was unmistakably of the wide range. "You want me again, Sheriff?" he asked in a throaty voice. "I've told you all I know about the . . . what happened. I'm doin' the best I can with the stock."

"That's all right," said Woods. "Sit down a minute. No? Well, Stagg, I've got a job on my hands, an' I thought maybe you could help me, although I can't say why I really should think any such thing." He glanced at Griffin who was leaning back studying Stagg's face as the foreman listened.

"We want to locate a man," the lawyer put in.

Stagg flashed him a look in which a vague antagonism lurked. "All three of you want him?" He turned again to the sheriff.

"Yes, all three of us want him," said Woods with a warning look at Griffin, "an' I 'spect every man on the Hanging X, including yourself, will want to see him. I'm talking about Gail Landon."

Stagg's expression underwent no change. "You want that squirt because he gets the big chunk . . . cattle, ranch, an' all?" he asked Woods.

"He gets everything 'cept what Nate left you an' a few of the old-timers," Wood repeated. "That's just about the chunk, I reckon."

"Little enough he left *me*, I'll bet," Stagg scoffed. He glanced at the papers on the table, and then looked at Griffin.

"He left you a thousand dollars in cash in a general bequest and a specific bequest of a hundred head of two-year-old Herefords," said the lawyer. "That isn't bad, Stagg. He also specified that three old hands were to have a small amount of cash each and lifetime jobs. The rest went to his widow, since he died first, and her will leaves everything to her son, Gail."

There was a calculating look in the foreman's eyes. "Two-year-olds, eh? I'd have to range 'em another year before I could ship 'em as beeves to get any decent money out of 'em. Who's going to pick 'em out?"

"Compton, here, and myself are executors," Griffin answered. "Gail is the other. You needn't worry about your bequests."

"*Humph.*" Stagg looked at the sheriff. "So your job is to find the boy wonder," he said in a voice slightly disdainful.

"That's it," Woods confessed cheerfully. "But he isn't exactly a boy now, Jim. He was pretty well growed up the last time I saw him, so I guess we can set him down as a man. He's probably gun perfect, too, but I don't hold that against him." He paused while he met the foreman's gaze speculatively. "As a matter of fact, I don't see as how any of us should hold anything against him, do you?"

"I don't hold anything against him," Stagg replied. "If I did, I wouldn't be fool enough to say so now with him owning the ranch." His thin lips parted almost in a smile. "But I don't," he added. "Do you know where he is?"

"I was going to ask you that, Jim," said the sheriff carelessly.

"Ask me?" Stagg's surprise was genuine. "How'd you expect *me* to know?"

"Because you're the foreman of the biggest ranch hereabouts," said Woods. "You're in touch with the Hanging X men. You don't keep many men around all winter, an' the rest of 'em float till it's time for the horse roundup in the spring. You've just got your outfit together, we might say, an' possibly you've took on some new hands. Any of 'em might hear something about Gail in the course of their roamings. They might tell you, or you might ask 'em. So I ask you if you've heard anything from the Hanging X crew, just as I'd ask Red Snyder, foreman over at the Bar Four, if he'd heard anything from any of his outfit. It's one way I have of getting information."

Jim Stagg frowned in the face of this logic. "I'd rather talk with you alone," he said bluntly.

"That's easy," said Griffin, rising and crooking a finger at the banker. "Compton, let's you and I go out and see if the cook has a coffee pot on the stove."

When the two had left the room, the expression on the

faces of the sheriff and the foreman changed. "You want the kid for anything?" Stagg demanded belligerently.

"Sure. I want him to come an' take charge of his property." The sheriff's tone was sharp, decisive. "That shootin' scrape was all cleared up before he left. He didn't have much use for Nate because he knew that Nate didn't like him. Stepfathers are apt to be that way, sometimes. I don't blame him for leaving, an' I reckon his mother thought it would be for the best. The past is wiped out."

"I didn't start askin' about him till Nate an' his mother were killed," said Stagg, "an' I didn't get any information till last night. One of the new men heard of him down in Wyoming last winter. He'd come up there from Arizona. My man hinted Gail had been travelin' with bad people."

"How bad?" Woods asked sharply.

"As bad as that Tarantula party, for one," Stagg answered.

"Don't believe it," the sheriff snapped. "If he was trailin' with Trantler . . . that's his name, or what he calls himself, anyway . . . I'd have had word through official channels before now. Besides, that spider cut-throat is a border bandit."

"Landon said he was goin' to travel when he left here," said Stagg. "A man can still ride from the line up north of here to the border down south or anywhere else on a horse."

"Yes, an' if Gail's as far south as Wyoming, he won't come up here to Montana," said the sheriff, frowning. "It would take too long to reach him by advertising in the newspapers there. I'm goin' to send somebody south to look for him. If you know anything more, tell me."

"That's all I've heard so far," Stagg said, frowning also.

"Look here, Jim, I know how you feel about having a

young boss," said the sheriff impulsively, "but you've got to make the best of it. You can be a help to him if you want to. Whether you like it or not, your bread is buttered by the Hanging X."

"An' I'm stuck here anyway till my hundred head are ready to ship," the foreman grumbled. "Who're you goin' to send south for a look-see?"

The sheriff raised his brows at the abruptness of the question. "I haven't decided about that," he answered coldly.

"Want me to lend you a man?" Stagg asked.

The sheriff rose. "Nope. You concentrate on the stock an' forget about other things for the time being. You need all the men you've got."

"Who'll I get orders from till Landon gets here?" Stagg demanded.

"From Griffin, the estate's attorney," Woods answered. "Now, suppose you see him later, Jim . . . after I've left."

When Compton and Griffin returned to the room after the foreman had gone out, Woods told them briefly what he had learned without mentioning the famous Tarantula.

"Who're you going to send to try and find Gail?" Griffin asked.

"Squirrel Cramer, but keep it to yourself," Woods replied.

"That sneaking rat!" the banker ejaculated. "Why, he. . . ."

"Will sneak around an' find him if anybody can," the sheriff replied. "I'll tell him the estate will pay him five hundred for his trouble, *if* he finds young Landon. You two better have a talk with Jim Stagg about what he's to do. Handle him easy. I'm ridin' back to Riverhead right away."

"I don't know Stagg very well," said the lawyer.

"Well, don't try to know him better straight off," the sheriff cautioned as he prepared to leave.

Fifteen minutes later he rode off from the ranch house to seek his prospective messenger in the county seat.

Chapter Two

In a bend of the stream south of the invisible boundary where the wind-swept prairies of Montana and Wyoming merged, a tumble of hills sheltered a grassy, flower-strewn meadow, with its silver ribbon of brook, lined with fragrant willows, berry bushes, and wild cherry trees. The noonday sun struck dazzling greens from the slopes of miniature ridges and embellished the whitewashed walls of three cabins with the sheer gleam of white marble. Several horses were grazing on the luscious grass and two men were sprawled in the shade of a cottonwood across the brook from the cabins.

"Trantler ought to be here soon," one of the men said in a listless voice. He turned cool, questioning eyes on his companion.

"Won't bother me any if he's late," observed the other.

The second speaker was a tall, presentable youth, rather dark, with bronzed, clean-cut features, hazel eyes that sparkled with an alert, adventurous light, even in repose, lithe with the natural grace of a made-to-order rider. This was Gail Landon, who had seen fit to change his name to Lantry as he followed the adventure trail away from the Hanging X.

"You don't talk as if you thought this business the chief's lined up for us is so hot," said Norm Spencer, who had spoken first. He was ten years older than his companion, heavier built, with an eye and manner that bespoke more experience. "Don't you like it, Lan?"

"I'm in it," said Lantry curtly. Although Spencer was the one man he had associated with to any extent during two years past, he never had told him his real name or mentioned his past. "After the raid I'm going to take a long vacation, Norm."

"Yeah? You'll double back for another big stake around the Fourth of July. The chief's took a liking to you. Know why?"

"Sure. It's because I'm young, keep my mouth shut, don't crawl in the dust at his feet, an' he thinks he can mould me into what he wants for further use. I'm just another likely looking tool to the Tarantula, Norm, an' that don't hold a very safe future for me."

Spencer chuckled. "Don't tell that to anybody else," he said, sobering. "The answer to my question is in your gun. That's what attracted the Trant's attention in the first place, when you got into that mess in La Junta. It was your gun speed that made him butt in an' get you out of there in a hurry."

"Maybe so. That trouble was wished on me, but I'm not makin' excuses. I reckon I'd've been killed if it hadn't been for him. I'll meet him that far. But I'm not goin' to let him dictate to me the rest of my life just because he helped me once."

"Don't worry," said Spencer. "He won't last that long . . . all your life, I mean. I was wondering if he hadn't had an eye on you down there that winter an' mightn't have wished that play on you himself."

Lantry stared. "It's possible," he conceded. "I never thought of that. I guess you're pretty wise, Norm. What do you think of this lay we got down in Graybolt?"

"The Big Horn Pleasure and Refreshment Palace," Spencer recited. "That's the answer. A big safe jammed with gold, silver, an' yellow backs. Why, that joint is a regular bank! It'll be one game where the big gamblers will lose, that's all. You needn't be squeamish about this job, Lan. The chief will leave 'em table stakes, an', when they find out who took 'em, they'll keep right on playin'." He laughed up at the blue vault of the sky.

"I guess you like this game," Lantry said with a tightening of his lips. "How long you been high riding, Norm?"

Spencer rose on an elbow and eyed him closely. "About ten years too long," he answered. "I suppose you think I ain't got much chance to get out of it. Well, I'm not lookin' for any. How about yourself?"

The younger man's eyes narrowed in cool calculation. "I'm goin' through with this raid, but I'm losin' interest . . . sort of, I mean." He couldn't tell his companion that he wanted to go up to the north range, now that he was so close.

But Spencer seemed to read his thoughts. "Got a girl somewhere?" he asked. "Just tell me to shut my trap if I'm gettin' too personal. You're young enough to be leery of this game, an' that means you're young enough to quit an' maybe get away with it."

"You're not more than ten years older than me, about thirty-five, I'd say," said Lantry, studying the other. "You could quit, too."

Spencer's gaze hardened. "You can't talk about quittin' as long as you're around this gang," he said slowly.

Shouts and curses sounded across the brook. The pair under the tree sat up to look. Two rough-appearing men came bursting out the door of one of the cabins, locked in each other's arms, and went down in a squirming heap on the ground. Others came out to watch the fight. The combatants went at it with all rules suspended as they gained their feet. Gouging, clawing, swinging, hitting, tripping, and biting, they fought, stirring up a cloud of choking dust. Their guns went spinning from their holsters, but they made no effort to recover them. Minutes passed before they were finally separated, bleeding and blowing, cursing aimlessly—satisfied. The group went back into the cabin.

"There's a sample of Trant's hold over his outfit," Spencer drawled. "That was a fight over a card game. He don't care about those things. But you remember they didn't try to use their guns on each other. Why? He would care about that."

"They didn't dare," said Lantry scornfully.

"You bet they didn't," Spencer agreed. "The chief don't aim to lose any man by having 'em kill each other off. If there's any hard shootin' to be done in the gang, he'll do it himself. They know it. Trant worships a gun in the right place, but not at the wrong time. He's groomin' you for a gun hand right now."

"He can't teach me anything in that line," Lantry flashed.

"Don't you think he can't. Maybe he can't teach you to draw any faster, or shoot any straighter, but he can teach you more different ways to shoot than you've got any idea of, boy. An' he can show you how to use a gun to get what you want without firin' it."

"Somebody's comin'!" Lantry exclaimed. "Up the creek . . . look!"

Spencer had spotted the two horsemen before the warning came.

"That's him with Slossom," he said quickly. "I reckon we're due to ride tonight."

Men came pouring out of the cabins as the outlaw leader and his companion drew up. They dismounted and disappeared into one of the cabins, leaving their horses to be looked after by others. In much less time than required for the speedy arrival, the scene was quiet again.

"Think we'd better go over?" Lantry asked. "I'm new to this thing, Norm . . . big business like this, I mean . . . an' I'm looking to you to sort of steer me."

"Don't you worry about that," said Spencer, with a short, mirthless laugh. "The old spider himself will do the steering. If he don't send for you to read you your part, I'll miss my guess."

Lantry frowned. "I expect this'll be hot stuff," he ventured.

"It'll be worse than that, if everything doesn't go off like clockwork," said Spencer with a grim smile. "We'll wear masks for this trick." There was a potent significance to this last statement.

"Will that help any?" Lantry asked, secretly glad he would be masked. He had been drawn into the business not altogether unwillingly, but to be recognized would stamp him definitely as an outlaw. He didn't believe anyone in that section knew him, save members of the band, but there was always the chance of being identified later.

"It'll impress the patrons an' make it so we can keep track of each other easily," said Spencer. "Trant don't need any because they spot him quick by his long arms an' those eyes of his, but. . . ." He ceased speaking as a voice called loudly across the brook.

"That'll be us," he said. "Let's go over. If the chief speaks to you, Lan, listen to him an' don't talk back."

"I didn't have any trouble talkin' to him three or four times before," the youth grumbled. Nevertheless, his eyes shone with suppressed excitement. It was nonsense like this that lured him further on the adventure trail.

One of the men accosted them when they reached the space in front of the cabins.

"The chief wants to see you in there," they were told as the man pointed an arm to an open doorway.

"What kind of a humor is he in?" Spencer asked lightly.

"Heavy as lead," was the laconic answer, accompanied by a leer. "Wants somebody to cross him so's he can spit lead at him."

"That means we're movin' fast," Spencer grunted.

The change from the dazzling sunlight to the semidarkness of the cabin nearly blinded them as they entered. They could see no one. The outlaw leader was sitting behind the table away from the light filtering in through the door and window. When they made him out at first, it was by the flickering greenish gleams in his eyes.

"Are you trailin' together?"

The cold voice cut through the room with sinister sharpness.

"We got something in common," said Spencer uncomfortably.

"An' how about you?" Trantler shot the question at Lantry.

"We're the youngest in the bunch," Lantry replied evenly.

"Then I'll use you together," the outlaw purred. "Maybe I'll send somebody along to watch you, but it'll be to see you don't make any mistakes an' not that I think you could cross me. Lots of 'em have thought of tryin' it. They're all kissin' daisy roots." The laugh that accompanied this sounded like the rattle of dry bones.

Lantry and Spencer said nothing. The latter appeared to

accept the outlaw's speech and manner as a matter of course, although he always appeared uneasy in the presence of his chief. There were only the three of them in the room.

But Gail Landon—now in the guise of Lantry—sensed an air of deadly seriousness he had never known before in his casual association with Trantler and the members of his band. This projected raid was to be the real thing, engineered and directed by the cleverest and most feared outlaw in the Southwest, a man who had won his dubious laurels by sheer daring, lightning draws and quick shooting, a certain amount of deplorable ruthlessness, and an agile mind with a twist for natural ingenuity in evading and outwitting posses, a worthy, if nefarious, match for the law.

The youth thrilled to the danger that would be involved; it would climax his adventures. Afterward—but the future was not clear as yet. The importance of events at hand overshadowed everything else. He could not know that pending events, and another of two weeks past, were to effect a change in him that would endure through a lifetime. An eager smile played on his lips and the outlaw noted it instantly. Trantler's eyes narrowed in calculation, not with displeasure.

"You same as told me you two hang together because you're the youngest in my bunch," Trantler said to Lantry—as he knew him by name. "You were down to Graybolt when Slossom slipped you the word to come up here. What did you think of the town?"

"Sheep headquarters," the youth replied with a note of disdain. "Supply point for sheepmen an' a heaven-in-hell for tinhorns an' such an' sundry that want to lay the dust in their throats an' ease the money load in their belts."

The outlaw's cruel eyes flickered with a light of admiration that was as quickly suppressed. "What'd you think of it, Spencer?" he asked, frowning.

"Just a tough stop," Spencer replied laconically.

"You know what I'm after?" Trantler flashed.

"I heard something about the Palace," said Spencer.

"Been there?" Trantler put the question to both of them.

Gail and Spencer nodded. Each was thinking to himself that Trantler knew where they had been and what they had done during their stay in the town.

"Here's what you're to do," the outlaw rasped. "You're to go down there so's to get there by night. Cross the creek an' swing into town from the east. It's the Palace you're to watch. Put up your horses an' get into a stud game where you can see the door to the private office. Get a look at every man who goes in or out of that door by midnight. I'm hopin' you're not too dumb not to know the law when you see it on two legs. If you see anybody who looks like he might be a gunman for the place, watch him. You can tell a gunman at first sight, Lantry, an' that's your piece . . . to spot 'em. Spencer can spot the others. Both of you got to use your heads. You're not well known there, for you ain't been there but once, as you told Slossom. Take it easy an' don't attract any attention. Don't forget what you see an' keep your ears parted wider than your hair. Sneak for the horses 'round midnight, an' somebody you know will meet you an' tell you what to do next." He paused. "Can you remember what I've said?" he snarled.

"You want us to spot any who might make trouble," Gail said.

"An' to see if the coast is clear at midnight," Spencer put in.

"An' be sure you do it," the outlaw snapped at them. "This is your first trick, Lantry, an' you better show me you're no kid. An' it's your biggest, Spencer, so it's your chance, too. G'wan, grab something to eat an' get started."

Half an hour later Gail and Spencer were loping across the billows of green prairie that was splashed with the colorful blooms of prickly pear. They hardly had spoken after leaving Trantler. Both were impressed by the outlaw chief's terse instructions and by his manner of delivering them. They had noticed, too, a growing tenseness among the other members of the band. There would not be more than fifteen men in the raid, they figured. It was bold business.

"The chief picked the right time!" Spencer called to Gail.

"Because the shearers are being paid off?" Gail asked.

"That's it. The Palace safe will be better'n a bank an' there'll be plenty around the tables."

"Who do you think will be meeting us at midnight?" Gail asked.

"Slossom, probably," replied Spencer. "We got an important bit in this, Lan. Reckon Trantler will want your guns close to him if it gets tough."

"Just my luck," said Gail, leaving the other to guess his meaning.

"Good luck, if you make it that way," Spencer told him.

"He'll have your gun, too, won't he?" Gail asked scornfully.

"Sure," Spencer answered. "But he wants to season you."

"Maybe he will and maybe he won't," Gail flared resentfully.

Norm Spencer reined in his horse and Gail did the same with a look of surprise at his companion, who was regarding him steadily.

"Look here, Lan," Spencer said impatiently, "don't you

feel right about this business? You act like you was sore because the chief picked you out for a leading part. You don't want to forget that I'm trailin' with you an' I'll get blamed if you. . . ."

"Cut it," Gail interrupted crisply, his eyes flashing. "I wouldn't start if I didn't intend to finish. But Trantler isn't going to season me as any gunman. He'd better teach me how to get results without firing first, like you said he could do. I've got the making of several things, I reckon, but none of 'em is a killer."

"That's the way I looked at it when I started." Spencer nodded soberly. "But I've had to put two notches on my gun. You might better put a notch on your gun in this game, boy, than put a stone wall or a noose between you an' the sun!"

"Do you think this is going to be that bad?" Gail demanded.

"I've got so I'm always ready for anything," Spencer replied grimly. "But I think you'd be right in a pinch, Lan. I'm ready to take that chance or I wouldn't pair off with you."

"Then let's get going," Gail said, riding ahead.

They reached the dusty, sun-washed town of Graybolt at dusk. After putting up their horses in the hotel livery, they went to a café for supper. By the time they had finished the meal, it was dark.

"We better go down to this Big Horn joint," Spencer suggested. The faint misgiving that had assailed him on the ride to town was gone.

"And attend to business," Gail agreed. His eyes were glowing with flickering lights of adventure, calm and keen anticipation.

The street was but dimly lighted by the yellow beams that shone through doors and windows. There were many pedestrians and groups of men about, for this was the end of the shearing season and the town was in the center of the sheep range. Merrymakers were plentiful. The street resounded with laughs, shouts, oaths, snatches of song, maudlin voices, and loud conversation.

"As good a crowd as a rodeo would draw, almost," Spencer remarked as they came to the Big Horn resort. "Trant can pick 'em."

The resort was a large room with a long bar on one side, sprinkled with gaming tables in the center, lined with wheels, crap tables, and a lunch counter on the other side, with private gambling booths in the rear. The place was well filled, most of the tables were occupied, the bar was lined two deep, spectators everywhere. Veils of blue smoke drifted under the hanging lamps and curled among the streamers of bunting that decorated the ceiling. Almost every conceivable sound that could be associated with such a rendezvous contributed to the bedlam.

Gail and Spencer picked their way through the spectators about the tables. They surged slowly toward the rear where the office was located behind a partition at the end of the bar. They had been in the place on their recent visit and already were familiar with it. They knew, too, that there was an open space in the rear and a row of open stalls where patrons left their horses. The rear door was reached through a, short, narrow hall between the private rooms where the big games were played.

They paused by a table where they could see the office door, and Spencer nudged his companion.

"See that short squirt at the lower end of the bar?" he said in a guarded tone. "He was hanging aroun' here every night we were here. Remember you said he was some kind of look-out?"

Gail surveyed the man Spencer had indicated.

"He's all of that," he said bluntly. "He's watching that office door like a hawk. He looks something like a hawk, for that matter, Norm. See that beak of a nose, the wrinkles beside his eyes . . . look at those eyes, Norm!"

Gail was suddenly conscious of the fact that he was staring straight into the narrowed, questioning gaze of the man he was describing. He looked away quickly, discomforted by the thought that his stare had attracted the look-out's attention and the man would be likely to remember him.

"He's wearing two shoulder guns or I miss my guess," Spencer said. "I'll keep my eye on him, Lan. He seemed to notice the way you was lookin' at him. You take a hand in a game where you can keep an eye on the office an' I'll squeeze in at the bar an' watch. I'll nurse my drinks, so don't worry."

Gail took a vacant chair at a table where stud was being played for moderate stakes and bought into the game. His vigil soon became disturbed by the realization that the look-out was interested in him. The man sauntered the length of the bar and wended his way back slowly through the groups of spectators around the tables until he stood with some onlookers across the table from where Gail sat. Gail played with the caution generally associated with a ranch hand who has a stake and intends to double it—at first. He was acting a part.

The look-out circled the table and finally stood behind Gail's chair. To all appearances Gail had not seen him, but Gail glimpsed Spencer watching the look-out through the medium of the mirror behind the bar. After a few hands had been played, the man trotted back to his post, evidently satisfied that Gail's stare had been by chance.

Gail won a pot, raked in the chips, and looked about with a smile that died instantly as his eyes met those of a spectator who had taken his place with those watching the game opposite.

This spectator was a slight man, with a skin like old parchment, bedraggled mustachio of dusty gray, but his small, eager eyes seemed burning with a message he was trying to convey without articulation. Gail was conscious first of a sickening feeling of disgust, then of anger, and finally was assailed by genuine concern.

He knew this spectator. The man came from the distant north range. Gail's attention had to be called to the game, so disconcerted was he by the new spectator's untimely appearance. As he played a card, Gail realized that the new arrival's presence in the town within a few hours of the impending raid was dangerous. He must get rid of him—get him out of Graybolt.

He passed with the next turn of the cards and rapidly counted his chips. His vigil on the office had relaxed, and, when he now shot a look in that direction, he failed to see the look-out. Nor was Spencer at the bar. He frowned at the eager spectator, who signaled him with eyes and an almost impenetrable beckoning nod of the head as he turned away with a backward glance.

Gail cashed in his chips, left the table, and strolled in the direction of the rear door at the end of the passageway between the private gaming rooms.

Chapter Three

Squirrel Cramer's agreement with Sheriff Will Woods in Riverhead had been tentative in the extreme. The small, shadowy wisp of a man with the restless eyes had promised nothing definite, had yielded no information which might bear on Gail Landon's possible whereabouts, and had exhibited a naïve cunning that the official had not suspected he possessed when he had been approached to serve as Woods's messenger in the search for the missing heir of the Hanging X.

He had agreed that five hundred dollars would be sufficient compensation, but had held out for one hundred dollars for expenses in advance—and got it. He had a furtive suspicion that Landon might be willing to double the amount the sheriff had stipulated as his remuneration for this exceptional service, although five hundred dollars represented a large amount of money to the Squirrel. It loomed twice as large in perspective. For Cramer's days of easy money had passed, and were gone forever.

He was a shady character who looked and lived the part. He still wore the gun that had served him well when he had ridden the high trails of outlawry. But the stiffness in his right fingers and the loss of one as the result of freezing had precluded any possibility of his ever being able to draw his weapon with his old speed again.

Without so showing the sheriff, he had jumped at the opportunity to ride forth in search of Landon. He had started quickly and had ridden fast. The day after leaving River-head he had picked up his first clue. Southward he had raced, and just two weeks to a day after leaving Riverhead he had arrived at Graybolt. Had Gail and Spencer dallied ten minutes over their supper, Cramer would have seen them in the café which he entered after they had left.

But Cramer did not know that Gail was in town. He had learned that one answering Gail's description had been there and he had expected to get some further word of him by visiting Graybolt. Consequently, when he moved among the throng in the Big Horn resort and found Gail there playing cards, his excitement over this swift accomplishment of his mission got the better of his judgment. He flaunted his message with eager eyes and all but gave himself away to the others standing around the table. He caught Gail's look of warning just in time and regained his normal senses sufficiently to wait a space and then follow Gail inconspicuously, so he thought, as the youth sauntered to the rear.

In the dimly lighted passageway Gail took Squirrel by the arm and drew him into an unoccupied room, the door of which had been open. He struck a match and lighted the lamp in a bracket on the wall near the door. Then he surveyed Cramer coolly. "You look like plain hard luck," he said in disgust.

"Well, my luck ain't been runnin' any too thick lately," the Squirrel complained. "But yours is holdin' good." His eyes flickered with returning excitement.

"This is the third time in two years you've chosen me," Gail said in a bitter tone. He eyed the older man speculatively. He had already hit upon a plan to get him out of town immediately. "I know what you mean by saying my luck is holding good," he continued with a frown, "but I'll have you know I make my own luck. Still, that doesn't mean I can keep it with you around," he said pointedly.

"You think I bring you bad luck?" Cramer asked, surprised.

"I've had bad luck every time after giving you a stake," Gail retorted sternly. "Just because you come from that north country up there, you seem to think it gives you the right to rake me for something every time you happen to run across me, and I don't like it."

"I'm sorry to bother you," Cramer whined.

"No, you're not!" Gail contradicted him. "You'd ask me for something even if you didn't need it because you think I'm easy. I'm going to give you one last stake with the understanding that you get out of town within an hour . . . just as soon as you can beat it. You won't bring me any luck being here."

"Maybe I've brought you more luck than you think." Cramer suddenly sensed that this remark wasn't exactly in good taste considering the news he brought. "Sheriff Woods sent me to look for you," he added hastily.

"Yeah? I thought my troubles were over up there."

"Maybe they've just begun," Cramer hinted with a smirk.

Gail grasped him by the shoulder and he made a futile stab at his gun, then looked foolish. "Stop talking riddles!" Gail commanded. "Why did Woods send you to look for me? Now, speak up, Squirrel, because I haven't much time to fool with you."

"Nate Martin is dead," Cramer blurted, his eyes glinting.

Gail withdrew his hand and stared. His eyes widened slowly. "Nate's dead?" He seemed unable to believe what he heard.

Squirrel Cramer found the breaking of the news uncomfortable. "Killed in a runaway a little over two weeks ago," he explained. "Nobody knew where you were an' the sheriff sent me out to find you. Nate was thrown outta the buckboard into the river an' drowned. He caught in some driftwood. Nobody knows just how it happened."

"How is my mother?" Gail asked quickly.

"She. . . ." Cramer hesitated. It was hard to get out what he had to say with Gail looking at him like that. But he saw that the youth was reading the truth in his eyes.

"She was killed, too." Cramer gulped.

Gail's eyes suddenly blazed dangerously.

"It's a lie!" he exclaimed. "You made that up thinking. . . ."

"Here's a letter from Sheriff Woods," Cramer interrupted, drawing a sealed envelope from a pocket and handing it to the youth.

Gail tore the envelope open and shook out the sheet of paper. He looked hastily at the signature, then read the brief note. His face went white under its healthy bronze. He folded the note, and put it away. "I'm sorry I said what I did about the luck, Squirrel."

"Oh, no, you ain't." Cramer chortled. "But maybe I did bring you bad luck, at that. Still it happened an' somebody had to find you an' tell you. What's happened can't be helped, an' now you're the owner of the Hanging X, anyway. You got to look at it that way, Landon."

Gail started at mention of his real name. His thoughts were whirling. What would he do? How?—the word kept repeating itself in his mind. He was staring hard at Cramer without seeming to see him. Gradually he realized he must get rid of Cramer first.

"You haven't brought me good news," he said slowly,

trying to regain possession of his numbed senses. "Perhaps you're right about the luck. Here, take this!" He drew a roll of bills from a pocket and thrust them into Cramer's greedy hand. "What I told you at first still goes," he said sternly. "Take that money and get out of town . . . quick!"

"Sure." Cramer chuckled as he stowed away the bills. "I'll go back up north. Woods promised me five hundred if I got the word to you. I didn't think it was hardly enough, but I had no idear you would. . . ."

"I'll make it as much more next time I see you . . . up north . . . if you'll go," Gail told him in a tone of contempt. He blew out the light in the lamp, and opened the door softly. "Get out and slope," he ordered. "Leave me alone in the dark . . . I want to think!"

As Cramer stepped into the hallway, Gail touched him on the arm.

"Go out the rear door," he directed, pointing.

Had he looked more closely, he might have seen the door he indicated closing softly even as he spoke. Instead, he stepped back into the darkened room. He scarcely heard Cramer leave, so tumultuous were his thoughts. He passed a hand over his eyes. The news of his mother's death affected him much more than he had disclosed to Cramer. In the brief moments during which he lamented his loss he upbraided himself for having taken to the trail he had followed these five years. He shook off his visible signs of grief by sheer will power. The sheriff had urged him to return at once. It was clearly his duty to do so, as the official had written in the note. But what about Trantler and the raid?

Gail now had no heart for the venture. He had met Trantler by accident, had trailed along with his band after the outlaw had assisted him in a time of trouble. It had seemed the easiest way out. But in so doing he had put himself under obligation to Trantler. Or had he? The outlaw leader doubtless so looked at it.

Gail, almost in a panic, thought of flight. He could steal out and ride away with Cramer—or by himself. Yes, he could go alone. He clenched his palms and pressed his lips to keep back an exclamation as he realized the futility of such a move. He would be missed first off by Spencer, and then by Slossom, who was probably already in town, since he was to meet them at midnight. They would search for him. His horse would be gone. It would be like Trantler to make inquiries, to try to find him. If he found him, what then? If he were to arrive on the north range?

Gail could not assume the risk. There was the memory of his mother. And there was the honor of the second man she had married. Yes, Nate Martin entered into it. Finally, there was Gail's new status and responsibility as owner of the Hanging X.

He had been born and raised in a small town on the "High Line", as the transcontinental railroad in northern Montana is known. He took to school just as he indulged the natural predilection of a healthy boy for the out-of-doors, which is unusual. He was thorough. The town was a shipping point for cattle, and his widowed mother and Nate Martin had been married there. The transition from town life to the comparatively free life on the open range broadened him and a spark of recklessness in his character was fanned into flame by new and venturesome contacts. He became an expert rider and skilled himself under clever tutelage in the use of his six-shooter. When he attained his majority, he was possessed of all the inordinate qualities of the "free rider" which he imagined himself to be. But there was still humor and keen joy of living in his eyes.

The news he had just learned had sobered him with the

greatest shock he ever had experienced. Whichever way he looked at his predicament, one solution offered itself as most logical. He must go through with this night's work, and, when the outlaw band separated afterward, he must ride away alone—to stay! This would prevent any suspicion and protect his future activities. After this one night, he must never see Trantler or the members of his band again.

As he went out into the big room of the resort, Gail Landon had so decided.

Chapter Four

Squirrel Cramer stepped from the rear door of the resort into the open space behind the building with a glow of exultation vibrating through his shriveled body. He glanced up at the stars with a twisted grin. He put his left hand in a pocket to feel the greasy smoothness of the roll of money it contained. This brought a gloating exhilaration and a cunning sense of expectation. Gail already had promised to pay him twice as much as Sheriff Woods was prepared to pay him for his services. He would manage to get more, and he would wheedle some kind of a steady job out of Gail. Cramer enjoyed a queer feeling of security. In his warped mind he considered he was fixed for the rest of his life. Moreover, having completed his mission expeditiously and successfully, he would have a vague edge on the sheriff.

He was so struck by these pleasant thoughts that he halted and stood for some short space of time in the starlight, motionless, then took off his hat to wipe his feverish brow. By this indulgence in personal satisfaction he gave a man who was concealed by the shadows of the horse stalls ample opportunity to study him and to observe the expression of avarice on his sharp face.

Any man happening to be there might so have observed him out of curiosity, but this man had been lingering in the passageway while Cramer and Gail had talked on the other side of the thin partition. He had slipped out the rear door just ahead of the Squirrel. It was Slossom.

Trantler's lieutenant had arrived in town a short time before. He had ridden boldly to the stalls in the rear of the Big Horn, and tied his horse. He was properly disguised by a heavy growth of beard, and it had been years since he had been in Graybolt. He did not think there would be any there who would readily recognize him, but still he had stolen into the resort by the rear door, his eyes and ears alert, and had caught the sound of Gail's voice when the youth had raised it to accuse Cramer of lying about the death of his mother and stepfather. Slossom had eavesdropped with no little success while appearing merely to loiter by the door, if he had been seen at all. In the semidarkness his eyes were smoldering coals of fire, but the flame in them was not kindled by any thought of loyalty toward Trantler. His duties, so far as the projected raid involved them, were clear, but his interest in Squirrel Cramer was personal.

A pair of rollicking horsemen galloping in roused Cramer from his brief reverie and started him walking rapidly to the street. He turned in the direction of the livery. His work in Graybolt was finished and he might as well get back to Riverhead. It also would be wise to humor Gail Landon by leaving town at once. It would be an excellent idea to be in Riverhead when Gail arrived, for then he could collect his fee from the sheriff (to be paid by the Martin estate) and receive the remainder of the double stipend from Gail. Cramer's narrow mind was running on a single track paved with money.

His horse needed a rest, but Cramer did not wish to run the risk of again encountering Gail in town. The one thing he desired most to avoid was Gail's displeasure. He paid for his horse's care and rode out of town in less than a half an hour after leaving Gail. He rode directly north.

The night air was cold, stars flooded the sky, and the plain was almost gray in their light; the wind was scented with the subtle perfume of sweet grasses. In the northwest the bulky dark masses of the mountains loomed, and straight ahead was a shadowy band of timber along a creek. Cramer could not resist the impulse to scan the denominations of the bills in the roll Gail Landon had given him.

He spurred his horse and galloped toward the timber ahead, where he proposed to stop. He was not far from town, but he was far enough so that he needn't be anxious lest he run into Gail. In his haste he didn't bother to look back to see if he was followed. He probably would have seen nothing to arouse his suspicions.

He dismounted on the grassy bank of the stream where he was effectively screened by the timber and bushes. He loosened the saddle cinch and permitted his horse to graze. He idled for a time, staring vacantly at the silver spangles on the ripples, looking up at the stars, walking about aimlessly. He took out the roll of bills several times, but he could not distinguish the numerals from the lettering upon them. For a brief moment he threw caution to the winds, struck a match, and peered eagerly at the bill on the outside of the roll. He extinguished the burning match quickly and drew a long breath in the pitch black that descended as the light died. He smiled and swore softly with elation as the stars broke out again. The bill he had seen by the flare of the match was a fifty dollar note!

Cramer's first conjecture was that Gail must have given him more money than he intended to let him have. In the excitement following the receipt of Cramer's important news, Gail might have acted rashly. He might even have handed over all the money he had! This thought stirred

Cramer's curiosity until his imagination was thoroughly aroused. There were many bills in the roll, and if they were all of such large denomination . . . !

The former outlaw couldn't stand it. He felt that he had to examine the money. The thought of night riders was speedily banished as he remembered how comparatively close he was to town. He decided to make a small fire and went about the task of gathering dry material for it with trembling hands. He could neither see the money satisfactorily nor gloat over it, to say nothing of feeling it and caressing it, by the intermittent flares of matches. So he built a moderate blaze. Aided by the light from the flames he secured more wood. At times Cramer's memory was apt to waver and he would lapse into a feeling of security such as had been his when he could manipulate his gun with extraordinary swiftness. As the years had gathered behind him, he had lost much of his inherent alertness. With the fire built he stepped back into the shadows of the trees and listened. A breeze whispered in the leafy branches, the flames crackled, and these were the only sounds he heard— both friendly.

Cramer really wanted to sit by the warm blaze and think and doze—*after* he had counted the money. He squatted near the fire and brought forth the roll of bills. In an instant he had forgotten everything except the notes he held in his hands. As he found the fifty dollar gold certificate to be merely a "cover" enclosing a wad of tens and fives, he cursed softly. Three hundred and ten dollars. In addition to the fifty, there were sixteen tens and twenty fives. Why, he had been cheated! If the bills had all been of the fifty dollar denomination, he would have had eighteen hundred and fifty dollars. He could even allow for a few scattered tens and fives and still have had fifteen hundred dollars if. . . .

The world and Gail Landon owed Squirrel Cramer money!

Cramer put the bills back in his pocket. After all, it was the best stake he ever had received from Gail. Twice before the youth had given him money—a hundred dollars each time—merely out of the goodness of his heart. Cramer had known him and had just naturally asked him for it. And he didn't know Gail very well, at that. Just a wild kid—that was the way he had thought about him. A good gambler and a high flyer. Perhaps he should be satisfied with what he had received. He would have to be, in fact.

"Hullo, in there!"

Cramer started to his feet as he heard the voice. He had been so occupied with his avaricious thoughts that his ears had failed to catch the warning sounds of an intruder's approach. As he turned, a horseman rode out of the trees.

"Where's this town around here?" the stranger asked, halting.

Cramer looked up at the bewhiskered face of Slossom and put him down at once as a sheep shearer on his way to Graybolt to celebrate.

"Straight south," he directed. "I reckon you mean the town of Graybolt." It wasn't surprising to him that the man was lost; sheep shearers were naturally dumb. Cramer's tone was patronizing.

"Glad to meet somebody who knows the country," Slossom said, feigning a friendly tone. "If you ain't got any kick, I'll get down an' warm myself a bit before goin' on. How far is it?" He dismounted without waiting for an invitation to join Cramer.

"Two, three miles," Cramer grunted with a frown. His visitor was a coarse-looking individual. No gun showed, but Slossom's coat was buttoned over his belt.

"I was closer than I thought," Slossom said with a

cramped smile. He held his palms over the fire and looked at Cramer.

Slossom remembered every word of the conversation he had overheard between Lantry, as he knew Gail, and this man, from the time Gail had exclaimed: "It's a lie!" The man before Slossom had said: "Here's a letter from Sheriff Woods." The letter evidently had proved something that this man had told Gail. Slossom remembered every word spoken afterward. He remembered particularly that Gail had called this man Squirrel and that the man had called Gail by the name of Landon. It was from this last that Slossom took his cue.

"You acquainted around here?" he asked.

"Some," Cramer replied gruffly. He didn't relish the intrusion.

"Did you ever meet up with a young buckaroo around here by name of Landon?" Slossom asked, looking at the other frankly.

The world tumbled into pieces about Squirrel Cramer's head. His original surmise that this stranger was a sheep shearer was swept away as if by the force of a powder blast. Suspicion, fear, distrust, and amazement all were commingled in the startled glance he shot at Slossom, and the latter noted this mixture.

"Can't say as I ever did," Cramer managed to get out.

"Tall, well set up, twenty-five or thereabouts, good-looking as billy-be-dog-goned with a laugh in his eyes an' a hand in his pocket," Slossom described, eyeing Cramer keenly.

But Cramer was shaking his head. He was not merely replying in the negative but shaking his head because he was in a dilemma. Why did that stranger ask about Gail? And how was he to find out why this man inquired about Gail

47

unless he acknowledged that he knew Gail?

"I heard he was in this town of Graybolt," Slossom explained easily, "an' I want to see him. Got a message for him. Thought if you was acquainted around here, you might have met him, that's all." He rubbed his hands and looked away from Cramer whose eyes were now eager and questioning.

A stranger with a message for Gail Landon? It might be the same message the sheriff had sent by him, Cramer thought impulsively. Had the sheriff sent out more than one messenger? Double-crossed? But, no, he couldn't be double-crossed, because he already had delivered the message, Cramer realized with relief. Still, it would be wise to learn more about this stranger.

"What did you say his name was?" Cramer asked. "In a way, the description you give fits a man I've seen around town."

"Good!" Slossom exclaimed. "The name is Landon."

"I believe I place him," Cramer said craftily. He didn't have to tell anything more than that he had met Landon. "First name is Gay, or something like that . . . Gail, I think."

"That's right." Slossom nodded. "Say, this is luck . . . to meet you this way. I was takin' a short cut an' saw a glimmer of your fire. Plain luck! I gotta find this Gail Landon. Do you know where he is?"

"That depends," Cramer answered wilily. "What do you want to see him about?"

Slossom frowned, then laughed shortly as he sized up Cramer. "Don't worry." He grinned. "I'm not the law, although I've got a message for Landon from it." He was groping in the dark as to the nature of the message, but he was mindful of what Cramer had told Landon to the effect that the latter now owned the Hanging X. What was the Hanging X? Where was it? These were the two things Slossom wished most to learn, for Landon was certainly Lantry, now of Trantler's band.

"You'll have to give me a better reason than that before I say any more." Cramer scowled. "What do you mean when you say you've got a message for Landon from the law?"

"I mean a message from Sheriff Woods," Slossom replied boldly.

The abrupt answer had the desired effect. Cramer's eyes flashed angrily. So the sheriff had sent more than one messenger!

"What is the message?" he demanded.

Slossom changed his tactics. He frowned deeply. "I reckon you know Landon, all right, by the way you talk," he said, "but why should you ask me that? You must be pretty close to him. Why should I be tellin' you when I don't know who you are?" He kept a level gaze on Cramer as he talked. "Say, listen," he said suddenly, "haven't I seen you somewhere before? Haven't you gone by some animal name? Squirrel, or something like that?"

Cramer's eyes popped. It was quite possible that this man knew him, or had seen him. It must mean that he came from the north range, and, if the sheriff had sent him out to look for Landon, as he had sent Cramer, he must know Landon, too. It was but natural he would be suspicious, same as Cramer himself had been mistrustful.

"My name . . . sometimes I'm called Squirrel," Cramer confessed. "But I don't remember you."

"You wouldn't," Slossom assured him. "I'm not sure of you yet. You've got to tell me where you come from before I'll spill any more to you."

Cramer now figured he had nothing to lose, even though

this second messenger might know everything. But his native caution did not entirely desert him. "I could ask you the same thing," he pointed out.

"An' I'd tell you where to go to," Slossom flared. "I guess Landon's in Graybolt, all right. I can tell that from the way you act. I reckon I'll push on." He straightened and hitched his belt. Cramer caught the gleam of the firelight on cartridge heads beneath Slossom's coat.

"I'm from Riverhead," Cramer said. "You come from there?"

"From there an' from the Hanging X," Slossom lied, watching to see what effect this misinformation would have on the other.

"From the ranch!" Cramer exploded. "So you an' the sheriff thought you'd put a smooth one over on me, eh? You must be a new hand up there who knew Gail was hanging out down here." He paused as a startling thought struck him. If this man knew so much, how did he come to be lost? "What's your name?" he demanded.

But Slossom was not minded to answer any more questions. He had learned what he wanted to know. There was a town called Riverhead and the Hanging X was a ranch. Whatever the message was, it must have been important. Cramer had stressed the fact that Landon, or Lantry, now owned the Hanging X.

"My name . . . to *you* . . . is mud," Slossom replied insolently with a leer. Taunted, Cramer, or Squirrel, as Slossom knew him, might be tricked into telling more, although Slossom had little time left.

"I reckon you're a four-flusher!" Cramer exclaimed, his hot temper getting the best of him. "If you think you're goin' to get anything out of Landon, you're crazy."

"Then I'll get it out of you," Slossom returned coolly.

Now he was baiting the Squirrel.

"Why, you. . . ."

Cramer's world went red with his sudden uncontrollable anger. He made that false pass for his gun. Even as he attempted the move, the folly of it struck him. It was to be his last blunder, but he realized this too late.

A croaking cry came from his throat as Slossom's hand whipped under his coat and out like a flash, his gun spurting flame and hot lead. Cramer plunged on his face into the fire.

Slossom pulled the lifeless form out of the blaze and went deftly through Cramer's pockets, taking what he found. Then he rolled the body into the stream, caught up his own horse, and rode swiftly through the trees to the open plain. It lacked forty minutes of midnight as he raced toward town.

Chapter Five

Gail saw no sign of Spencer or the look-out who had been watching the office door when he returned to the big room of the resort. More than likely the look-out had left the place and Spencer had followed to keep an eye on him. Gail strolled toward the front entrance, looking about the room to make sure they were not there. As he considered the prospect of again sitting in a game, it suddenly struck him that Squirrel Cramer would likely return to Riverhead and tell Sheriff Woods where he had delivered his message, that he had found Gail in Graybolt.

Gail stood still while he thought over this new angle that might embarrass him at a later date. News of the raid would most certainly carry across the Montana line. If it became known that Trantler had been responsible, word would surely be broadcast by letter and circular to every sheriff in Wyoming and Montana. The information that the notorious outlaw was this far north would warrant the warning.

When, and if, Sheriff Woods received the news of the raid, would he not immediately mark the coincidence that Cramer had found Gail in Graybolt on the very night of the raid? Of course, this would prove nothing, but Gail didn't fancy the thought a little bit. It would be easy enough for Cramer to say he had found him elsewhere. If he was leaving town at once, he might never learn about the raid. In any event, Gail thought it would be wise to instruct

Cramer to say he had found him in southern Montana somewhere. For that matter, it was really necessary. Gail might reach Riverhead before Cramer.

He decided to find the messenger before he had an opportunity to leave town. He went out the front entrance and started up the street. Gail didn't know how long he had remained in the darkened rear room thinking, but it was long enough to enable Cramer to get to the livery and for Slossom to follow him and ascertain his purpose. It was merely chance that Gail did not meet Slossom as the latter hurried back to the rear of the Big Horn to get his horse to follow Cramer.

Instead, Gail met Spencer, and this was disconcerting to his plan. It meant frustration of his scheme to tell Cramer to conceal the meeting place. It meant more than that, as Gail speedily discovered.

"What'd you leave the game for?" Spencer asked in an excited undertone. He fell in with Gail, and they walked along together.

Gail realized instantly that his presence on the street required an immediate and satisfactory explanation. For a brief moment he trifled with the thought of taking Spencer into his confidence, but this would be taking too long a chance. Spencer was the one man in the band he knew best and the only one he could trust to a certain extent, but he decided he could not trust him this far.

"I followed a man out who I thought took that look-out's place," he told his companion. He described Cramer slightly.

"One of us should stay in the place," was Spencer's only comment. "I edged out behind that two-gun party an' heard him called Jordan. He went to the hotel, an' I came back. What you goin' to do?"

Gail wasn't sure whether there was a subtle hint of irritation in Spencer's tone or not, but he chose to call the turn. "I'm going to walk up the street and back," he said. "I didn't like the looks of the *hombre* I saw and I wouldn't mind getting a closer squint at him. Suppose you go back to the Big Horn and wait for me."

Spencer slackened his pace. "Sounds sensible to me," he said. "Don't lose any time followin' a nightmare. We got to go for our horses at midnight an' meet somebody, like the chief said. We can monkey around an' get nervous if we suspect everybody we see." He turned away.

Gail went directly to the livery. A gold piece helped him here, and he learned that a man answering Cramer's description had procured his horse and ridden away some little time before. As he walked back toward the resort, Gail resolved to reach Riverhead in advance of Cramer at all costs. He might even overtake him on the way. In one respect he was satisfied, for he was glad the man had left before the raid. But Gail could not shake off a vague feeling of misgiving. It seemed an evil omen that he should be bent upon this mission which now loomed clearly as one of Trantler's spectacular forays. It would create a tremendous sensation. Posses would comb the plains and mountains. Gail realized thoroughly that as soon as possible after the raid, or during the confusion if anything unscheduled should happen, he must get away—far away—away to safety. Nothing could be allowed to hinder his escape.

His face was set in firm lines of determination when he went into the Big Horn. He saw Spencer sitting in a game near the rear of the room. He sought out a place at a table nearby and began to play. It lacked about an hour of midnight. Jordan, the look-out, came back to his place near the office door and Gail saw him talking there with a man who had been pointed out to him on his recent visit as the proprietor. Furtive glances convinced Gail the two were engaged in casual conversation.

Gail began to win, and despite the load on his mind the game caught him in its spell. The news Cramer had told him grew hazy and even now there was a glimmer of doubt in his mind. His chips swelled into tall yellow and blue stacks and his vigilance relaxed. He looked up suddenly to catch a frown from Spencer. A glance at the clock showed the hands at five minutes to twelve. Midnight! Spencer was cashing his chips, and after the next hand Gail proceeded to do the same. He let Spencer go out first, and then followed him casually. As he walked, he noted that the look-out was standing at the lower end of the bar, but he wasn't drinking.

The room was packed and only a limited number appeared armed. Gail suspected that they wore weapons that were not in plain view. It was a noisy throng, with a majority in various stages of intoxication. There was an uproar all along the bar where patrons were packed three and four deep, knotted into groups. It was the busiest hour of the night for the augmented force of employees on shift. Gail marveled that Trantler should select such an hour for his raid. He was to learn that the outlaw's decision was not one of sheer daring.

The inner door of the private office was open to the space behind the bar. As he flung a last look over his shoulder, Gail glimpsed the huge safe in the office, its heavy outer doors flung wide. The proprietor passed before it.

Spencer was waiting for him near the alley that led between buildings to the open space and horse stalls in the rear of the resort. As Gail met Spencer, a voice addressed them from the shadows that cloaked the alley. They recognized the voice as Slossom's and stepped into the alley at the soft-spoken command.

"Is everything clear?" Slossom asked.

"There's a squirt of a two-gun look-out named Jordan perched at the end of the bar," Spencer replied. "An' Lantry, here, saw a queer one."

"Who was it?" Slossom asked Gail sharply with a burning look.

"I dunno," Gail drawled. "I followed him out and lost him. He isn't there now." He had to look up as he spoke to Slossom because of the man's height. He liked Slossom, with the small, wide-set eyes, hard face, beetling brows, and protruding chin, less than any of the members of the outlaw band. He distrusted him, also.

"Yeah?" Slossom sneered. "Well, watch him if you see him again. Now, listen!" He leaned down to glower at them. "You two have been picked because you're fast an' straight with your guns. You go in shooting, understand?" He gave them no time to think about this other than to digest it. "Here's why," he continued briskly. "Lantry, you take the hangin' lamps in the rear . . . the first three. Shoot 'em out! Spencer, you take the next three. Shoot 'em out! Your first job is to shoot out those six lamps. Then close in by the office an' cover the work of the chief. If anybody makes a move, put him out like the lamps!" He paused to let this sink in. "I'll go in first with some men an' get behind the bar. We move the crowd back against the tables. You come next with Trantler an' the others. There'll be men in front an' back. This thing has to be done quick while the sheep are pickin' the wool out of their brains. It'll be almost dark in there when you've done your work. The light'll come from the office door an' the lamps up front. If the mob starts shootin', shoot back . . . for keeps. But don't fire at a man in a mask, for we'll all be masked."

As he paused again he drew two black handkerchiefs of generous size from a coat pocket. He handed one to each of them.

"Use those," he said gruffly. "If anybody's got on a colored bandanna, it won't be one of the bunch. Remember that. Go get your horses an' ride right in behind here like you'd just arrived. The rest of the crowd'll be here quick enough. Then you'll listen to Trantler. If you don't mind what he says, you'll find out why he's named after a bad spider!"

A chuckle rattled in Slossom's throat as he hurried away in the shadows toward the end of the alley.

"C'mon," whispered Spencer, taking Gail's arm. "This is goin' to be the daddy of 'em all, I'm sayin' to you." The fact that Spencer was so excited impressed Gail.

They hastened toward the livery to get their mounts. The street was nearly deserted now, as the celebrants were all making merry indoors. A quarter of an hour later, when they rode into the space behind the Big Horn, they found the vanguard of the band already there.

Slossom was moving about giving orders in a low voice. There was no talking. The men dismounted swiftly and the horses were bunched, with a man looking after them or left standing separately at the hitching rails, where each man could easily find his own in a hurry. Slossom told them where to put their horses.

"Over on the left," he said to Spencer and Gail. "You'll ride out the main street straight west. Don't forget." It was both an order and a warning. Several more men rode in, and one spoke sharply to Slossom. It was Trantler, and his manner of speaking left none in doubt as to who now was in charge. His commands were crisp, concise, and clear, and there was no misunderstanding them. Slossom moved to the rear door of the resort. Trantler stepped quickly to Gail and Spencer.

"We'll go in right behind Slossom," the outlaw chief said in a low, vibrant voice. "Shoot those lights out soon as you can get a bead on 'em. Then stand in front of the office while I'm inside. Follow me when I give the word an' start out."

His eyes seemed to flash all over Gail's person at once. "You got two guns?" he asked.

"One," Gail replied.

"Here's another," Trantler barked, handing him a second weapon. He raised his hand and a brief silence fell upon all.

In this breathless moment it seemed to Gail, as the men crowded together, that there was no system—yet there was methodical precision in Trantler's every move and in the apparently casual actions of his experienced men. With this organization operating in perfect unison about them, Gail and Spencer were virtually impelled into doing what they were supposed to do because it was the only thing left *for* them to do! It was as if each small group had been told what to do individually and nothing else. Nothing was said about an emergency.

As Gail glanced about at the men, he hurriedly thrust the extra gun into his belt and took the handkerchief Slossom had given him from his pocket. Quickly he tied it about his face just under his eyes. All the men were masked with the single exception of Trantler. Gail had been watching him so intently he hadn't seen the others don their masks. The outlaw leader's eyes were burning into him again and Gail sensed that Trantler had deliberately held up proceedings to teach him a lesson. It made him feel foolish for a moment. Then his eyes blazed with the determination to show the outlaw he was not a fool.

Trantler's hand came down. "Into it!" he commanded in a harsh, ringing voice.

Slossom's hand was on the door as his chief spoke. In a moment he had opened it, and he and the three with him slipped swiftly inside.

"Go ahead!"

Gail and Spencer could not mistake the order intended for them.

Spencer leaped inside and now Gail was into it, indeed. With Trantler at his shoulder, he followed Spencer. Already there was a lull in the turmoil at the lower end of the bar. As they burst from the passageway into the crowded room, Gail caught a single glimpse of Slossom and the three with him driving back the groups near the office. Then Spencer's gun crashed into the sudden stillness and a lamp splintered and went out.

Gail's gun roared with Spencer's and five shots smashed the other hanging lamps that rained glass and dripping flame on the tables, players, and spectators. *"Back to the wall!"* Trantler shouted above the din as he dashed for the office where the treasure reposed in the big safe.

A gun barked sharply in the front of the room and another lamp went out. Gail saw masked faces, other members of the band, up there. Then the throng turned and moved in a jam toward the wall.

Lamps, glasses, and bottles crashed behind the bar, and, as Gail reached the office door with Spencer, he saw Slossom and his men behind the bar each with two guns leveled across it at the panic-stricken customers who were jostling, struggling, pushing, and falling against and over one another in their mad effort to crowd away.

Chairs were kicked aside and broken, tables were overturned, scattering chips, cards, and money to be kicked about the floor, roulette, blackjack, and crap lay-outs crumbled before the impact of the mass. The smoke cast a saffron pall over the dim scene of wild disorder and the crowd cowered before the masks and threatening guns of the raiders. "Turn your backs to the bar, you sheep!" Slossom thundered.

The mob twisted and turned. They were shouting and cursing now. "A hold-up!" "Outlaws!" The cries swelled to a din. But all this confusion merely served to make the work of the raiders easier.

Gail heard the sounds of rough voices, the scraping of feet, and the clanging of metal coming from the office behind him. A masked man ran behind the bar, emptying the contents of cash boxes into a sack. Trantler was superintending the gathering of the loot.

Next instant came the unexpected. From the dark mass of the crowd, packed along the shadowy wall, came a spurt of flame, and the room seemed to rock with the report of the shot. The bullet shattered a pyramid of glasses on the back bar. With the whine of the hot lead still singing in his ears, Slossom yelled and fired. This was the signal for a volley from the men with him.

A shrill, prolonged shriek of protest and terror seemed to come from the throng as if from a single powerful throat. Then the crowd broke for the doors, heedless of the guns that covered them. Some of the mass surged to the rear, another portion swept toward the front entrance, and a wave billowed on the floor where men flung themselves to avoid expected bullets.

Slossom and the others came leaping over the bar just as Trantler rushed out of the office.

"Go out the front!" Trantler roared, emptying his gun

over the heads of the onrushing mob.

Spencer was shooting, too, and now the guns of Slossom and the others thundered. The wave hesitated, broke, and rolled back. The men who had been with Trantler poured out the office door. They carried sacks weighted with plunder. A fusillade now rocked the front of the building and the last of the lights went out there, leaving only the light shining from the office and a glow in the passageway in the rear.

"Out of it!" Trantler shouted hoarsely.

There was a rush for the rear, the outlaws taking the order to be every man for himself. In a moment the narrow passageway was jammed. Then came the struggle to get through to the horses and away before the whole town could come down upon them.

Gail had been caught off balance and flung aside by the headlong rush. He was in the rear as the band squeezed through into the passageway. He looked around with a wild thought of mingling with the crowd in the darkness and being left behind to escape alone. At this moment a figure darted across the light shining from the office door. Gail recognized Jordan, the look-out. Jordan's gun came up.

Gail leaped for the passage, now cleared, as a bullet whistled. The extra gun came out and Gail fired once. A shadow tumbled in the beam of light and Gail dashed through the passageway and flung himself out the door.

Horses were plunging, rearing, snorting as the outlaws darted among them, mounting hastily. Gail stripped the handkerchief from his face and stuck it in a pocket as he ran for his horse. Spencer already was in the saddle, waiting for him. Spencer's voice came to him.

"Here!" Gail cried. "I shot the look-out!"

Next he was riding madly out of the black mouth of the

alley, his brain on fire, no thought in his head save for flight. As he galloped with the others into the street, he saw men pouring out upon the narrow sidewalks from the various resorts, rooming houses, and hotels. The night air was filled with shouts, the din punctured by a few scattered shots. The riders offered poor targets, for they were leaving fast and only those spectators from the Big Horn knew what the confusion was about.

Gail turned his horse up the street and galloped toward its end and the west road. Spencer was with him; Trantler loomed in the saddle on a big horse ahead; there were others who carried the sacks containing the spoils. Trantler kept his eye on the treasure-bearers just as he watched everyone and everything else. The others of the band took the opposite direction and rode east, headed by Slossom, to confuse immediate pursuit.

They reached the road and raced westward for a mile, Trantler and those with him. Then Trantler veered to the northwest where the mountains reared their black bulks into a sea of stars. They slackened their pace. Soon the flying shadows of those who had left by the east road came into view, circling wide to the north of town, riding hard to join the first string of outlaws with which Gail rode.

Slossom arrived first and galloped his horse close to Trantler. The chief and his lieutenant spoke briefly. All the band was safe.

They rode on. The full pounding of flying hoofs was all that disturbed the quiet of the night.

Organized pursuit would require time. No official of the law would send inexperienced men out to search for this band, nor would any official send a small posse. To read sign and track the outlaws on the prairies and gumbo flats and trails would require daylight. The raiders were thus assured of several hours' start.

Some of the men began to speak to each other in gruff voices.

"Keep your tongues behind your teeth!" came Trantler's hoarse command from forward.

The voices died. Gail was riding close to Spencer. The foothills were creeping toward them as if the mountains were shaking out the dark folds of their flowing robes of shadow. The horses had settled to a steady pace and miles were covered smoothly.

Chapter Six

The first glimpse of dawn brought a gap in the higher hills into sight. The band was riding slowly in tumbled country, with the gray expanse of plain behind them showing only when they surmounted a ridge. There was some scrub timber, much brush, thick undergrowth along trickles of stream, rock outcroppings and boulders. The riders were following a thread of trail that wound over ridges, through gullies and ravines, and climbed steep slopes to drop off into shale or porphyry or casual clumps of jack pine.

Presently, in the clear light of day, they swung over from a high ridge to a miniature divide, directly opposite the yawning gap and overlooking a wide ravine that led to its mouth. Trantler posted a look-out on this point of vantage before they descended into the ravine where there was water, grass, an abandoned cabin and corral.

"We're making a stop here," Spencer told Gail as they loosened their saddle cinches after dismounting. "There's nobody close to us and it's a good place to stand off a posse. Two men could keep an army outta that gap. We'll have breakfast and maybe the divvy."

The horses were permitted to graze on the luscious grass in the ravine. Gail and his companion found themselves with nothing to do after they had attended to their mounts. Older hands were expertly engaged in the quick preparation of a meal. The sun flooded the green hills in a golden burst of glory.

Gail and Spencer kept somewhat apart from the others, as had been their wont for the past month. They rolled and lighted their cigarettes. Spencer was slyly watching his companion, for Gail was frowning and his eyes appeared worried.

"You say you plugged that look-out, Jordan?"

"Had to," Gail answered crisply. "He started shooting at me."

"I suppose you're going to let that keep you awake nights," Spencer scoffed. "He wasn't the only man shot when things blew up."

"He's the only man I ever shot."

"Shot dead, you mean? Maybe you didn't kill him at that. Boy, the only thing I've got to say is that with your draw and aim it's a wonder . . . well, you're lucky." Spencer's tone was grim, as if he were thinking of his own unfortunate record.

"Look here, Spencer," Gail said impulsively, "I've got to get out of here . . . away, I mean."

"Sure. So've I. We've all got to get away, so far's that goes. The chief will probably hold us together a while yet . . . today, maybe . . . in case we should be followed fast. Then we'll split. Did last night's business cool your feet or your brains, which?"

Gail ignored this sally. "I've got to get away at once," he said, looking steadily at Spencer's blond face and deep, blue eyes.

"Uhn-huh." Spencer nodded with a curious look at his friend. "Just like that, eh? Why, Lan, you're not the kind to get cold feet this easy. I can see you haven't froze on us by the look in your eyes. I mean it. You said something yesterday about takin' a long rest. What is it? You can tell me. I'll bet it's a girl!"

Gail's eyes flickered just enough to cause Spencer to believe he had hit upon the truth. In fact, Gail almost was on the point of telling him that his mother and stepfather were dead. He caught himself just in time against this risk.

"Have it your own way, Norm," he said, "but I've got to beat it. Suppose I told Trantler so in as many words?"

"He'd probably tell you to go to hell," Spencer drawled. "You might make a sneak but you'd lose your divvy. You want what's comin' to you, don't you?" For Gail to say he didn't care anything about his share of the loot would make Spencer curious to the point of open suspicion and bring a flood of questions.

"I could get it later," he evaded.

"You don't know where we're goin' to meet next," Spencer pointed out. "An' if you sneak away, it'll make Trant suspicious that you're hedging. That would be dangerous. Stick around and see what happens. Girls like you all the better if you keep 'em guessing."

Gail swore under his breath at this bit of homely philosophy. Then both became aware that Trantler and Slossom were moving about among the men. A few moments later the chief outlaw and his aide approached them.

It was impossible for Gail to keep out of his gaze a hint of what was in his mind as he returned Trantler's scrutiny. There was a snaky quality to the outlaw's keen glances from one to the other of them. Slossom merely stared coldly and appraisingly.

"Knocked off that look-out, huh?" Trantler fairly spat the words at Gail.

"I guess so," was the answer. Gail didn't flinch, however.

"There mustn't be any guessing when you shoot with this outfit," Trantler gritted through his teeth. The man had a fearsome personality even in his most amicable moods.

Gail saw a smirk on Slossom's face, although it's doubtful if the man himself knew it was there. The youth's eyes flashed instantly. Revolt swelled within him until it burst forth in words he had had no intention of speaking. "If we're through, I want to slope," he told Trantler boldly.

The outlaw's eyes narrowed, but he showed no surprise or anger. "Gone cold?" he sneered. "Where you want to go?"

"On my own," Gail said, with a note of defiance in his tone.

"He's got a girl," Spencer put in to smooth matters out.

"Yes?" purred Trantler, his teeth gleaming. "Wants to get away to talk to a woman. When you tell a woman anything, Lantry, you tell the law! You stay with me."

There was a girl about whom Gail was thinking at that very moment, one he remembered rather vaguely but favorably. This was Doris Keene, daughter of Matt Keene, who owned the big Bar 4 ranch next to the Hanging X up north. A vision of the girl bloomed faintly in Gail's brain. Instantly he thought of other things, of the tragedy he had learned about the night before. He must reach Riverhead before Squirrel Cramer could get back there to forestall the messenger saying where he had found him. Time—every minute!—counted.

"The raid's over," he told Trantler steadily. "I did my work. I shot out the lights and I stopped the look-out when he started to pour lead into our backs as we were leaving." Spencer had grasped his left arm and was squeezing it in warning but Gail paid no attention to him. "I don't know what the rest of the outfit figures on doing, but I've got business of my own to tend to. I can get my part of the divvy when I see you again. I told you I had to leave when. . . ."

"Shut up, you pup!" Trantler roared. "You're through with your work when I say so. If you start for your horse before I tell you, I'll drop you in your tracks!" His eyes were glittering balls of jet and green.

Gail saw Slossom shaking his head at him. Spencer had drawn away. Others of the band were watching, attracted by the outlaw leader's harsh voice. He held back the hot answer that was on his tongue. But he looked dangerous and confident as he thrilled to the realization that he was not afraid to draw with Trantler.

"If you've got any sense, you'll keep your mouth shut," Slossom told him over Trantler's shoulder.

"If he opens it again, I'll fill it with lead!" Trantler barked.

Gail was wise enough to desist. A gun play at this time with Trantler would get him nothing, even though he should emerge victorious. He would have to fight the band, with the possible exception of Norm Spencer. He had too much at stake. But what he didn't put in words he tried to convey by his eyes.

"He ain't convinced!" Trantler ejaculated hoarsely, taking a step toward Gail.

But Slossom put a light hand on his chief's shoulder. "Let the cub cool," he said. "Remember, this is his first big business."

"An' he thinks his own puny affairs are more important!"

"He's young," Slossom compromised.

"All the more reason why he should be careful!" The

outlaw made as if to speak to Gail again, but shook his head impatiently and turned away. "Remember what I said," he flung back, with a dark look.

But Gail had decided to make a break for it at first opportunity.

He and Spencer had coffee and sandwiches of bread and meat with the others. They ate silently. Gail knew Spencer disapproved of what he had done and he surmised that Spencer felt he might be an object of Trantler's displeasure himself as a result. Gail determined to forestall this, if necessary, by having an argument with Spencer before he tried his break. While Trantler's suspicions, and those of Slossom and Spencer, might have been aroused if Gail had left before the raid, it was different now, and with a general alarm out and posses scouring the country, Trantler could hardly stop to search for Gail once he had disappeared. Gail almost hoped a posse would get close so he could effect his escape in the confusion of the race for mounts and the getaway, or fight. His opportunity came from a wholly unexpected quarter within half an hour after his altercation with Trantler.

Slossom came out of the cabin where he and Trantler had been and motioned to Gail and Spencer.

"Get your horses," he ordered, speaking to both of them, "and ride up to relieve that look-out. Tell him to come down for something to eat and orders. Keep your eyes on our back trail. Come down like all fire if you see anything out of the way." He waved an arm toward the horses and left them, going back to the cabin.

Gail Landon's heart leaped, first in exultation, then with misgiving. The order must have come from Trantler, but why should the outlaw chief give him this chance?—because he thought Gail would not double-cross Spencer and leave him to bear the brunt of his anger? As Gail caught up his horse, he knew his chance had come and he was prepared to make his break. But he would protect Spencer from any suspected implication.

Norm Spencer, too, was disturbed by the coincidence that the two of them should be sent to relieve the look-out on the divide above the ravine, but he attributed the order to Slossom, believing that Trantler merely had told his lieutenant to send somebody to relieve the look-out. Knowing Slossom well, as he thought, he surmised that the man wouldn't care if Gail got away or not. One less man would increase the shares of the others in the plunder, and it might be that Slossom was a bit jealous of Trantler's interest in his youthful protégé. In any event, the business was up to Slossom.

They lost no time in riding up the divide, where Spencer gave the outlaw who had been left there his orders. The look-out started for the floor of the ravine at once.

From this high vantage point the foothills, mountains, and the sweeping prairie lands below met their gaze in a mighty panorama. A cool breeze, filtering down through the mountain stands of timber, blew across the divide. There were birds, and a cock-ruffed grouse strutted proudly in the sun spangles between two silver firs. The green waves of plain, gold-spattered where they merged into the blue of distance, gave no sign of human movement as of horsemen; a silver ribbon of river gleamed in its emerald setting—spring and a universe of soft beauty, with the mountains standing vigil.

Gail looked at Spencer after they had surveyed the scene.

"Got any idea where we're going to meet up next?" he asked.

"I heard it was the Cotter Ranch, six miles west of Libbyville, July Second," replied Spencer without looking at him.

"This puts me in a hard spot," said Gail quietly.

"It puts me in a harder one," Spencer said coolly.

Gail had noted the steep trail by which they had climbed the divide earlier in the morning. To the left of it was a shale slope that apparently broke where some pines trailed across it, a dangerous short cut. Gail had hunted much in mountain country and his horse was capable.

"It isn't just a girl, Norm . . . I mean the reason why I have to go. I wish I could tell you more."

"I don't want to hear anything," Spencer said in a hard voice.

"Then . . . *so long!*"

With the last words, Gail literally kicked his horse into the shale. Down they went, the horse sinking, sliding, floundering in the treacherous fine rock, Gail kicking out of the stirrups and flinging himself from the saddle as the animal fell, plowing its way toward the line of trees. A choking cloud of dust rose, obscuring them. From above came the sharp staccato of pistol shots and bullets whistled overhead. The horse pushed a boulder out of its path and the big stone swept over the brink of a precipice and crashed like a thunderbolt upon the granite outcroppings below just as horse and rider, uninjured save for minor cuts and bruises, came upon firmer footing, where the trees stalked across the shale. Gail caught up his horse and picked his way to the trail.

Chapter Seven

There was no search for the youthful recruit known as Lantry by the outlaw band. Spencer reported that Gail's horse had bolted and rolled down the shale slope with its rider to plunge over the cliff in the rim rock. Slossom who appeared after Spencer's futile shots—signals, Spencer called them—accepted the explanation. In fact, Spencer thought Slossom accepted this view of what had happened almost eagerly. Trantler merely verified it with a few crisp, short questions. Spencer's answers could hardly be denied since he had been with the band most of three years. But Spencer later found he could not easily dismiss his erstwhile companion from his mind.

Every mile that Gail Landon rode carried him farther away from the name of Lantry and the band of outlaws he never expected to see again. Nearly five years had passed since he had accepted one thousand dollars from his stepfather, Nate Martin, owner of the Hanging X, and had ridden away at nineteen on the then glittering high trail of wild adventure. He had learned much, but he had not absorbed the pain he now hoped time would dim, if not blot, from his mind. He felt keenly the loss of his mother, the former Sally Landon, who Nate Martin had married and who had met death with him in the fatal runaway. He hoped to reach Riverhead, the county seat near the Hanging X, ahead of Squirrel Cramer, the sheriff's messenger. But Cramer's body was swishing in the stream down near Graybolt—as only Slossom knew.

Gail was prepared to assume his real identity the day after his escape from Trantler when he crossed the Montana boundary, but none questioned him. Thirty-one times he crossed the fords of rivers and streams in the next ten days. He rode the green waves of prairie northwards— north by east—past pink and purple buttes, between straggling ranges cast off by higher mountains, across dull, brown, sun-baked gumbo flats, through river breaks and badlands, in and out of dusty, gray cow towns shaded by graceful cottonwoods, and finally brought up one late afternoon in the bunchgrass with the cool shadows of Riverhead a mile distant in the dying gold of the sun.

Gail took his time covering this last mile to town. His gaze continually roved eastward in the direction of the Hanging X. There were cattle in sight but they belonged to smaller ranches closer to town. He debated what he should do first in Riverhead and decided that, since it had been Sheriff Will Woods who had sent Squirrel Cramer with the message, he had best visit the official in his office at once.

He experienced a thrill as he trotted his horse into the main street. He would be a power on this range now, a man of influence in town. For the first time it was brought home to him that he was very wealthy. But much of his wealth was on the hoof and it could dwindle like magic with improper handling. Yes, he was riding into the lap of responsibility. He braced himself in the saddle and threw his head up as he turned in at the livery.

Sheriff Woods looked up from his desk as his office door opened, stared as his visitor entered, then rose and walked around the desk to extend his hand.

" 'Lo, Gail," he greeted heartily. "You've filled out from

a boy to a man in the years since I saw you last. You look powerful fit and handsome. A good clear eye. Did Cramer come back with you? . . . or did you hear some other way? I sent Squirrel Cramer to find you. Sit down." He drew up a chair for the new owner of the Hanging X.

Gail breathed deeply with relief as he took the chair. So he had arrived ahead of Cramer. Good!

"No, Cramer didn't come back with me, Sheriff. I rode fast. I gave him some money and he might have hesitated somewheres to grease the green-topped tables with it. He couldn't have kept up with me, anyway."

"I thought he'd take you for something," the sheriff growled. "I told him they'd pay him five hundred from the estate if he found you quick enough . . . before anybody else did."

"He couldn't tell me very much about what had happened." Gail was glad the sheriff pressed no inquiries as to where Cramer had found him. "I feel pretty bad about my mother and I didn't have anything against Martin. I didn't fit in with his scheme of things, I guess."

"You'll have to fit in now, Gail," Woods said seriously. He told Gail about the tragedy at the ranch in which Gail's mother and stepfather had lost their lives. "Your mother died last and left you everything," he finished. "She fell heir to it by your stepfather's will when Nate Martin died first. You get everything 'cept a thousand cash and a hundred head of Herefords . . . two-year-olds . . . which Nate left the foreman, Jim Stagg. Three old hands got two hundred cash each and lifetime jobs. You've come into a big property." He eyed the young man in front of him keenly as he said this.

"You got anything against me, Sheriff?" Gail asked abruptly.

"Not a thing," Will Woods declared. "I'm not even asking you where you've been or what you've been doing these last four years. I'm wishing you luck and I'll be watching to see you make good."

This expression of goodwill impressed Gail. It might be the first evidence of his new and important station in the locality. "You'll remember I had some trouble before I left."

"Times seem to have changed somewhat during my last four years in office," Woods drawled, his eyes shining kindly. "We don't have much trouble any more. Time was when they called this Trouble Range, but I haven't heard it called that for years. The law is more particular now. I'm forgetting a lot of things because I don't believe they could happen again."

Gail was quick to discern that this subtle statement was a potent warning.

"What do you think I should do first?" he asked.

"If I were you, I'd see Frank Griffin, the lawyer. He and Henry Compton, the banker, are the executors of the estate, with yourself, of course. He knows the legal angles and he's been keeping an eye on the ranch. He put Stagg in charge down there, which was the only thing he could do. Maybe you better not ride down to the ranch till morning. Do you want me to go with you? No, I see you don't. Well, there's no reason why I should. I'll take you over to Griffin's office. He knew all of Nate's business and your mother's, too. Nice fellow, Frank, and square as they chop 'em out."

Gail had never met Griffin that he could remember. He looked at the lawyer's strong, ruddy face, met his straight gaze, felt his powerful handclasp, and liked him at once. He harbored none of the hatred of the law that obsessed the regular members of Trantler's band. He greeted the attorney cordially.

"How old are you, Landon?" Griffin asked.

"Twenty-four, with a birthday coming up in December."

"And inheriting more than ten thousand dollars, maybe twice that, for every year of your age," said Griffin, pursing his lips. "Quite a load," he added as if to himself.

"I never expected to get that ranch,"—Gail frowned—"but now that I have it, I'll do my best to take care of it. Sheriff Woods said you were attending. . . ."

"Yes, yes," Griffin interrupted with a wave of his hand. "I've been looking after matters and I'll attend to all the legal details. I want to get a little better acquainted with you before we go into a business session."

"I'll be going," said the sheriff, turning to the door of the office. "Gail, I'll leave you here with Griffin. I'll be in my own office 'most all evening if you want me for anything."

"The sheriff tells me that things are more law-like and orderly around here now," Gail said when the official had gone. "I reckon he was tipping me off that he wouldn't stand for no rough stuff." He eyed Griffin closely.

"I suppose a man in your position could have a time without getting in jail," said Griffin dryly. He looked at Gail quizzically. "As owner of the Hanging X you're an important figure here, Landon. You're too important to cut up ordinary-like."

"I never was ordinary," Gail ventured a bit grimly. "Since you attended to Nate Martin's business and my mother's, I want you to attend to mine. I want you on my payroll just the same as if you were working on the ranch."

"You're retaining me, you mean." Griffin laughed. He sobered quickly as he noted Gail's serious look. "As your attorney I wish to ask you a question."

"Shoot," Gail told him with a nod. "Maybe I'll answer it."

"You've been away going on five years," Griffin said slowly. "You've covered a lot of country, I understand. You're young and able, with the spirit of adventure in you. I can see it in your eyes. You've had a lot of experiences and you're the sort that doesn't go in for soft things. Have you got much to cover up?"

"Plenty," Gail confessed, looking his questioner straight in the eyes.

"I thought so," said Griffin, leaning his elbows on his desk. "Do you want to tell me about . . . anything?" He put the question casually, but his look was one to inspire confidence.

"No. Not now, anyway." Gail was on his guard instinctively.

"Have you killed anybody?" Griffin asked sharply.

Gail started in his chair. "No," he answered steadily. It was true that he didn't know if he had killed that look-out down in Graybolt or not, and, even if he knew he had, would he not be a fool to tell about it?

"I asked that question because I've heard about your proficiency with a six-gun," Griffin explained mildly. "Such skill may be handy at times, but it's dangerous. But I'm not here to preach, and I can see that one doesn't get acquainted with you in a minute." He looked at his watch. "I suggest that we go over to my house for supper, Landon. We can talk more comfortably there. I want to tell you all the circumstances of your mother's death, and that of your stepfather, and about your property. I want you to have all the facts, naturally. You'd better stay in town tonight and I'll go out to the ranch with you in the morning. Will you come along?"

"Sure," said Gail, rising. "But. . . ." He studied the lawyer's face a few moments. "I don't know just why it is, but I want to ride out to the ranch alone," he said in a determined voice.

Griffin looked up at the tall youth. He wasn't surprised, but there was no hint of sentiment in Gail's voice or gaze. A whim?

"Very well," said the lawyer, getting to his feet. "Let's go."

Gail rode into a glorious June sunrise next morning when he was early on his way to the ranch. The green reaches of prairie were splashed with the pink and yellow blossoms of the prickly pear. Meadowlarks chirped their cheerful treble of song flitting on swift wings along the road. The air was sweet and a light breeze laved that open land under the great blue arch of cloudless sky. Spring was caressing the semi-altitudes. In ten days the rains would be due. After that, the blistering, scorching summer and a sea of yellow grass.

A buckboard in which two men were seated rattled past but Gail knew neither of the two occupants. They nodded to him and he nodded back. He threw a look over his shoulder and caught them gazing back at him. An hour out of town he passed two riders but they were strangers. He wondered how many were left at the ranch who he knew. There would be Stagg, of course, and Mrs. Birch, who had been Nate Martin's housekeeper before he had married and who had stayed on. Then there was Luke Denan, the old hand mentioned in Nate's will for a lifetime job. Denan had first taught Gail to draw. There had been Chuck Clark, a rising young cowboy who had completed the job of teaching Gail how to use his weapon until the pupil had surpassed his instruction in speed and accuracy. Gail remembered some of the other hands. Four years, even to one at his time of life, seemed a long time.

Then there was that wisp of a girl with the big eyes—fifteen she had been when he left—that Keene girl from the Bar 4 who had teased him. Doris, her name was, pretty girl but too smart. Gail smiled in the wind. No girl could be too smart for him now.

As the sun mounted, he passed other riders, a man in a spring wagon, a stage, but he knew none he encountered. On this ride he realized poignantly how alone he was; no near relatives were closer than Minnesota, and he knew little about them. He wondered just where he would turn for friends. It seemed fitting, in his imaginative mind, that he should ride to the vast property he had inherited so unexpectedly alone.

At last he saw the willows and cottonwoods about Eleven Mile Spring where the road forked and a branch led southeastward to the Hanging X. Eleven Mile marked a corner of his domain. Beyond lay the Bar 4 range and deeded acres equal almost to his own. He decided to stop at the spring, and drew rein in the shade under the cottonwoods just as a rider cantered in from the east.

Gail found himself staring into a large pair of eyes that seemed like deep brown wells alive with light. There were soft cheeks below those eyes, a dainty nose with a saucy, upward fling, and cherry lips. "Hello, neighbor," he greeted, as the girl pulled up her horse.

"It's Gail Landon!"

"And you're Doris Keene." He smiled, his hat sweeping low in a gracious salute. "Grown up and more than pretty. I'm glad to see you."

"I'm sorry you have to come back like this," Doris told him in genuine sympathy. "I mean, I'm sorry because of what happened." She was inwardly noting the fine figure he made in the saddle, his clean features, his hazel eyes with the dancing lights in them. "You've grown up, too, Gail." She forgot rumors she had heard.

"Enough so I can take my misfortunes with common sense," he said a bit sternly. "I've been thinking for days while I was riding back. I've got to be sensible about it all because it can't be helped. I was figuring that I didn't have a real friend around here, unless it might be old Luke Denan at the ranch. But maybe you're still my friend." He looked at her hopefully.

Doris smiled in a way that caused him to catch his breath. "Of course, I'm your friend, Gail," she said. "Why shouldn't I be? We were kids together." She arched her pretty brows daintily as if what she said was a mere statement of fact.

"You were going on sixteen when I left," he said wonderingly. "Now you're twenty and a lady. I could pick you out of all the girls in the world by your eyes."

"He's learned flattery!" Doris mocked. "If you meant that as a compliment, I mean. You used to get mad at me. You rode away and left me at the Teton picnic."

Gail's troubles went sailing. "You never forgot that." He grinned. "Well, you rubbed me pretty hard that day . . . too sassy, I thought. Something you didn't know is that I rode back to get you and saw you going home with another *hombre*. I stayed mad for a week."

Doris laughed. "Secretly I used to be afraid of you," she confessed with an amused toss of her head. "I suppose you've been around a lot." She paused for Gail's comment, but none came. "I've been away to school winters," she volunteered.

"How'd you happen to be riding here?" he asked. "Are you going on to town?"

"Gracious, no! I often ride over here to the spring. It's just a good ride from the house."

"Why, it must be ten miles," Gail said, surprised.

"I like to ride and I like this spot. This is the neutral corner, you know. Dad and Nate Martin nearly had a feud over this spring once. Only the two ranches can use it in emergency. It's just dawning on me that you own the Hanging X now."

"I didn't expect it and it doesn't seem real yet, Doris."

"Father said he was going over to see you when you got back."

"He used to tolerate me," Gail said wryly. "Told Nate once that I was a necessary pest. What does he think about me now?"

"Dad's all right," Doris evaded. "He doesn't say much. He felt awful sorry about Nate Martin and your mother. He hasn't seen you in a long time. He said, if he could be of any help, he would."

"Well, now, that's fair enough." Gail smiled. "I wouldn't be surprised if I needed some help, too." He looked at the girl speculatively. "Maybe I should say I'll need encouragement," he supplemented.

"You were always pretty sure of yourself, Gail."

"I'm just as sure now," he told her earnestly. "And one thing I'm particularly sure of is that I've got the most beautiful neighbor of any rancher in the country. Now, don't flare up. That was just an appreciation, Doris, and you've got it coming. I reckon a lot of fellows, who haven't seen as many girls as I have, have told you the same thing, one way or another. One trouble with me has been that I say what I think, usually. I'm not so good at cute talk."

"Do you tell all the girls you know what you think?" she taunted.

"There you go!" he accused. "But you can't make me mad any more. I've known a lot of girls . . . plenty of 'em. I've flirted with 'em, played around with 'em, left 'em liking me or cussing me, I didn't care which. But I never made love to any of them."

Doris's eyes were wide. "Am I to assume that you're making love to me?" she asked blankly.

Gail considered this question so gravely that Doris burst out laughing. "No, I don't think so," he said, flushing through his tan.

"I hope not . . . so soon," she said, then frowned lightly as she sensed a foolish meaning in her words. "I hope you're not going to be like the rest of them," she added hastily. "I'm pestered tired by men who say they want to marry me, Gail. I'm glad I've got a friend to tell my troubles to." Her eyes were sad. In this sudden, unexpected mood she appeared more attractive than ever.

"I should think they would," Gail said bluntly. "Why, it doesn't seem like four years or so have made much difference to us. I used to tell you my troubles. Suppose we meet now and then and swap troubles." His gaze was luminous, twinkling, boyish.

"I'm riding back to the ranch," Doris announced primly. "I'll tell Father you're back. Mother will likely tell him to ask you over. She always liked you. She used to say you were wild but harmless. I wish you lots of luck."

"Wait a minute!" he exclaimed as she made to turn her horse. "Shake hands, Doris. I'm glad to see you again!"

She hesitated, flushed slightly, then leaned from the saddle and felt her hand in his warm grasp.

"I'll be seeing you again," he promised.

He watched her out of sight on Bar 4 range. Then he watered his horse and turned down the road toward the

Hanging X home ranch, six miles to the southeast, in the rich bottoms of the Teton.

He was scarcely out of sight when a horseman broke from the trees above the spring and galloped eastward, leaving a feather of dust to ride the wind.

Chapter Eight

It was Luke Denan, his lean, leathery, weather-beaten face puckered into an intricate pattern of countless wrinkles, enlivened by his broad smile and bright blue eyes, who welcomed Gail Landon in the courtyard of the Hanging X ranch buildings as Gail swung down from his horse near the big barn.

"I'm shore glad to see you," old Luke said with feeling as he grasped Gail's hand. He took the reins in the stubs of his left thumb and fingers—the hand that had been frozen "tight" in the service of Nate Martin in the early years—and looked up with no uncertain measure of pride at the tall youth before him. "You look fit, Gail," he added convincingly.

"I'm glad to see you, too, Luke," Gail told the pensioner. He felt a surge of confidence in the presence of this wise old hand. For Luke always had been loyal to Nate Martin, had enjoyed his trust, and there was no faint hint of deceit in his make-up, for he was outspoken, truthful, and as reliable as time is sure.

"I'm going to have a little talk with you before I see any of the other men," Gail said. "Who's here at the ranch?"

"Just me an' the hands who're workin' the bottoms," Luke replied. "I've got one rider helpin' 'round the barn. Had to fight to get him, but I reckoned you'd want a man handy to carry messages when you came. Been expecting you for two weeks. An' there's Missus Birch." He pointed toward the rear of the ranch house.

Gail turned to meet the elderly but active housekeeper who bustled out to him, voicing her welcome in a motherly, mildly excitable voice. She was of Southern extraction, and capable.

"Shoo now, Denan, and put the master's horse up," she warbled. "Bring his saddle pack in the front. Come in, Gail. We'll go in the front as becomes you. Every day I've been looking for you . . . always with something ready for you to eat. What a man you've grown up to be! Well, we need a man here now. Your poor mother and stepfather . . . I'll take you out where they're buried . . . and you mustn't worry . . . grieving won't run this ranch."

He had taken her arm as they walked toward the yard and the front of the big, rambling ranch house with its wide porch almost smothered in vines and morning glories.

Mrs. Birch talked on as they circled a clump of lilac bushes and mounted the steps. "I've fixed up the front spare room for you. It looks out on the yard with one window toward the bunkhouse. I didn't think you'd want the big corner room where. . . ." She caught herself as Gail opened the screen door and they stepped into the large, comfortable living room, with the little room that had been Nate Martin's office leading off from it, the wide staircase winding up from it, and the open door of the dining room revealing a table covered with white damask and set for one.

"I'll bring you some coffee right away," Mrs. Birch chirped. "Then you shall have a man-size breakfast in a jiffy. Lena, the kitchen girl, is helping me. I'm so glad you're back, Gail."

"The coffee will be enough, Missus Birch, thank you," Gail said, smiling faintly. "I had breakfast in Riverhead before I started out here. I can wait till noon."

"Very well," said the housekeeper, appearing slightly disappointed. "Maybe you want to tidy up a bit. You look dusty. But you know where to go. It's a wonder Griffin or some of them didn't think to come out with you. Well, I'm glad you're back."

"I wanted to come alone, Missus Birch," said Gail firmly, "and I told them so. Yes, I guess I'll wash up." Thus Gail Landon's homecoming was accomplished.

Late that afternoon Gail called Luke Denan into the house. He waved him to a chair in the living room while he rolled a smoke. "Where's Stagg?" he asked, snapping a match into flame.

"He's down in the Corner lookin' after the two-year-olds," Luke answered. "He's paying more attention. . . ." He stopped suddenly, tugging at his drooping mustache in agitation.

"Yes, yes . . . go on," Gail prompted, lighting his cigarette.

"He's down there in the Corner lookin' after the younger stuff."

"Paying more attention to them because he's heard he was left a hundred head by Nate Martin." Gail nodded. "Is that it?"

"I guess you know all about the will," Luke countered.

"Griffin read it to me last night . . . read both wills, I should say. Nate left you two hundred and fifty cash and a lifetime job, Luke. But he didn't say anything about you staying at the home ranch in snug quarters with a warm barn in winter. I can put you down in the Corner by the badlands to keep cattle out of the brakes." Gail looked steadily at the old man as he said this.

"An' it might be a good place for me!" Luke blurted. "I'm still spry an' I ain't askin' no favors." He glared bravely.

Gail laughed. "I'm not going to do any such thing, Luke. But I want you to answer me when I ask you questions and give me any information I wish. I have to depend on you more'n you think. Does everybody around here know about the wills?"

"Reckon so, lad. That lawyer feller, Griffin, told Stagg and Missus Birch. Guess he had to. I'm not a spy, Gail, my boy."

Gail looked at him quickly. He had caught a note in the old hand's tone that indicated Luke didn't altogether approve of things in general—of the way Stagg was running the ranch, perhaps.

"I'm not taking any one man's word for anything right at present," Gail said with a frown. "Is Stagg working the stock the way Nate usually did in the spring?"

"From what I hear he's changed things aroun' a bit, but I don't know, because I haven't been out on the range," Luke answered readily. "He hasn't been here in a week. Last time he was in, Red Snyder was with him an' he didn't stay hardly an hour. I reckon he's waitin' to see you."

"Is Snyder that Bar Four foreman who used to be over there?"

"That's him . . . Keene's man. He was on his way to town an' rode through with Stagg this far."

"More gumption since Nate died, eh," said Gail with a trace of annoyance. "I can't remember that any of the Bar Four outfit ever came on this range much except a visit from Matt Keene, the owner, once in a while."

"They didn't . . . while Nate was alive," Luke said succinctly.

"So customs are changing now?" Gail lifted his fine brows. "This ranch is going to be run as nearly like Nate conducted it as possible," he added stoutly. "He made it pay and I'm going to try to do likewise. And I'm not asking any help from the Bar Four that I know of as yet."

Old Luke's eyes sparkled. "Nate was a smart stockman," he ventured. "Still, there's no harm in Snyder ridin' through. But Nate never had any use for him."

"How did Nate and Matt Keene get along?" Gail asked.

"Got along fine after they patched up their difficulties 'bout ten years ago. Matt came to the funeral an' acted like he felt right sorry. I heard him tell Stagg if he could be of any help to let him know, and Stagg said he guessed he could run things as he had been doing."

Gail shrugged with a thoughtful look. "That wasn't any too friendly on Stagg's part," he commented.

Luke had nothing to say to this.

"Stagg was decent enough with me . . . most of the time," Gail said. "Of course, I ran pretty much with the men as I liked, but he taught me a lot about working cows."

"You were a top hand," Luke declared.

"Well, almost," Gail agreed. "I was only nineteen when I left and I'm not very old now. But the situation is changed, Luke. Now I own the Hanging X. Owning the ranch and being its stepson, you might say, is different. I'm more than top hand now." His face grew grave as he said this.

"That's right," said Luke, gazing at him curiously.

"I'm telling you this for a reason," Gail explained soberly. "You're much older than I am. You've had much more range experience. I understand my stepfather was not above taking your advice on occasion, and I'm not above it, either. So far as the rest of the outfit is concerned you're sort of in charge here at the home ranch. But you're on the payroll as my . . . er . . . assistant. When I ask you for advice, I want you to think hard and give it to me straight. That's a more important job than being a barn man, Luke. This is all I have to say now."

Gail had finished supper and had gone out of the house to look at the fading glory of the sunset when Jim Stagg galloped in and dismounted in a cloud of dust. The foreman called to Luke to take his horse and walked straight to Gail, holding his right hand outstretched.

"Hello, Gail," he greeted loudly. "How's the cowboy?" He wrung Gail's hand in a terrific grasp. "You're sure man-size now, all right!"

"How are you, Jim?" Gail responded. "I was going to send for you in the morning. I just got here a few hours ago." He was puzzled because something in the foreman's manner indicated that he had known of his return soon after he arrived.

"Oh, I heard you was back," said Stagg somewhat airily. "A Bar Four 'puncher sighted you an' sent over the word. I've been looking for you, of course, an' I'd like to have had a man in Riverhead waiting, only I've needed 'em all on the range. Did Cramer get the word to you? It was a tough break for Nate an' your mother. Nobody knows how it happened. Horses are frisky an' scary in the spring."

The young ranch owner could not help but see that Jim Stagg was brimming with confidence, somewhat excited but very sure of himself, and suspiciously cheerful. He nearly gave the impression of being pleased because of the dreadful thing that had happened. Gail's own manner cooled perceptibly. "Come in the house," he invited.

As they entered the living room, Stagg took off his hat. "The only times I've been in here was on business with the

Old Man," he said, seating himself comfortably.

"You're here on business now," Gail told him, "with me."

Stagg started to frown, but grinned instead. "Sure. I'm not forgettin' you're the big boss, Gail. I was glad to see you get the chunk. The old man might have done a little better by me, but I'm not complaining. I suppose you saw Griffin in town?" His eyes punctuated the question.

Gail stood by the table, staring at his foreman. He realized that Stagg had tolerated him—in a small way, catered to him—on the ranch before, but that was when Nate Martin was the power in charge. Now Stagg's attitude seemed to be patronizing and subtly complaining about the thousand dollars in cash and hundred head of stock that Nate had left him! Gail resented this more than anything else.

"I think Nate did pretty well by you," Gail said. "A good many times a foreman isn't remembered half so well, if at all."

"Smoking Moses, you don't think I was just a foreman, do you!" Stagg ejaculated. "Why, I came on here when I was a kid, you might say. Do you reckon I was gettin' forty a month when the rest was gettin' thirty just because I was good at chasing dogies?"

"What was the extra ten for?" Gail inquired curiously.

"I was a good cow thief!" Stagg blurted. "Oh, I guess you could hardly call it that. But I was good at findin' strays an' puttin' the Hanging X iron on 'em. That was nuthing. All the old-timers did that."

"So you think it wouldn't have hurt Nate none to have left you more?" said Gail, lighting a cigarette.

"I've got to wait a year till the two-year-olds are heavy enough to ship," grumbled Stagg. "Good thing he didn't leave me shorthorns."

"I'll give you a thousand dollars and a hundred head of beef stock tomorrow if you want 'em," Gail said quietly.

Stagg stared at the younger man as though he never had seen Gail before in his life. "What's that got to do with it?" he demanded.

"It disposes of the matter you were speaking about," Gail replied coldly. "If you want to take up my offer, all right. Otherwise, I don't want to hear any more about it. If you're going to stay on here, you'll receive what you have coming in the regular way."

"Stay on here? How could I go? I'd be a fine sort to leave you flat! Sure I'll forget about the . . . the other. I guess no matter what you give a man, he'll kick. That's one reason why I keep a tight rein on the outfit."

At best, this seemed a peculiar way of explaining Stagg's attitude—so Gail thought—but it was further evidence of Stagg's supreme confidence in himself and his sense of security in his position. Gail found himself nettled. Instead of an expressed desire to co-operate, Stagg seemed to have a program of his own mapped out. He regarded Gail as someone who was just going to be around! Leave him flat, indeed!

"Where did you ride in from?" Gail asked.

"I've been down in the southeast the last few days," Stagg said matter-of-factly. "I'm ranging some stuff down there this year."

"Nate didn't use the Corner much, did he?" Gail asked casually.

"In a lot of ways Nate was old-fashioned, you might say," was Stagg's answer. "There's good grass in that southeast Corner an' I'm using it. Snyder's put in some men an' cattle, too, down there, an' we're ridin' 'em in off the badlands."

"Snyder didn't used to put in with us much, did he?"

"That's old stuff, too," said Stagg with a wave of the hand as if he would dismiss the subject. "He an' me have called everything bygones. I never really had anything much against Snyder."

"But Nate didn't use that range, did he?" Gail persisted.

"No," Stagg confessed with a frown. "But that doesn't stop me . . . us . . . from using it now, does it?"

"Old-fashioned," Gail mused. "This is an old ranch, Stagg."

The foreman gave him a queer glance as he heard himself called by his last name. At this moment Gail certainly looked older than the twenty-four years he boasted. This, in turn, nettled the foreman. "This is one of the oldest ranches in the north range," he said.

"They tell me it's probably worth a million," Gail said evenly. "Nate Martin must have been a good stockman to build such a property."

"Sure he was," Stagg conceded, considerably puzzled. "I never said he wasn't, did I? I just said. . . ."

"I'm going on the theory that Nate Martin knew his business," Gail interrupted sharply. "I'm going to range the cattle and work the ranch as nearly like he did as I can. That's common sense. We'll string out the herds as he strung 'em out at the different seasons. You know the routine and I'll learn it fast enough. You take the stock out of the Corner and put it where Nate would have had it at this time of year. We've got plenty of range, haven't we?"

Stagg now stared as if he could hardly believe his own ears. "I thought you'd want to take a look around before you started giving orders," he blurted angrily.

"I'm going to begin looking around tomorrow," Gail informed him. "I want range conditions as near as possible to what they would be if Nate Martin were here. I want to see all the herds and I want a count to tally with the figures Griffin gave me. Griffin will be out here in the morning, so you better stay in tonight."

"But I told 'em I'd be back tonight," Stagg remonstrated.

"They'll probably understand that I asked you to stay in," said Gail dryly. He threw his cigarette end into the fireplace impatiently. "You might as well face the facts, Jim. I'm back here now, not as a kid riding free on the range, but as the owner of the ranch. I feel as if it'd been left in trust to me. I've been through a lot more than you think, but this is the toughest proposition I was ever up against. I'm going to try to use my own best judgment, but I'm wide open to advice and suggestions, and I want the co-operation of every man in the outfit. I've got to have it! In order to get it, you and the others must understand that I'm in charge. All I hope is that I can do two things right for every one thing I do wrong . . . at the start."

Stagg had a belligerent expression on his face. "If you can do that, you'll be a wonder!" he snorted.

"Then let's hope I'll be a wonder," said Gail grimly. "If you haven't had supper, Luke will see you're fixed up in the cook shack. I'll see you in the morning."

Stagg left the house with rage surging through his powerful frame. He met old Luke near the door of the bunkhouse.

"That young squirt said you'd see about supper," he snapped. "Hop to it, old cracked bones, an' see that it's hot!"

Luke Denan smiled cheerfully for the second time that day.

Chapter Nine

Sheriff Will Woods arrived at the ranch early next morning in his buckboard with the attorney, Frank Griffin. Jim Stagg, who had been fuming about, wrathful and sullen because he hadn't seen Gail since the night before, saw them come and was on hand to welcome them as Luke took charge of the team.

"Where's Landon?" Griffin asked.

"Dunno," Stagg replied. "Holed himself up in the house after supper last night an' hasn't shown since. Sleeping, probably." The quality of his tone caused Sheriff Woods to glance at him sharply.

Before more could be said, Gail appeared and led his visitors to the front porch, where there were chairs screened from the bright sun by cool, green vines. "You're here early," Gail told Griffin. "And I didn't expect you out, Sheriff, but it was good of you to come."

"What's the matter with Stagg?" the sheriff asked bluntly as they sat down close together.

"Doesn't like the idea of having a young owner for a boss," replied Gail. "He as much as told me he was running the ranch last night and I had to tell him I was the works and needed co-operation. I've been letting him stew around this morning to think it over."

"You didn't discharge him, did you?" the sheriff asked quickly.

"No. But he's got to change his viewpoint or I will."

Sheriff Woods frowned and looked at Griffin.

"He was close-lipped with me," said the lawyer with a shrug.

"Well, Frank, whose business comes first?" Woods asked Griffin.

"Yours, I should think," Griffin answered with a glance at Gail.

By now Gail was aware of a certain solemnity in the manner of the two men. They seemed to avoid looking at him directly. Their faces were grave. He felt a momentary choking sensation of fear.

The sheriff took out a cigar, thrust it between his teeth unlighted, and began to chew it—a sign that he had much on his mind.

"Gail, how long since Squirrel Cramer gave you my message?"

Gail's fears fled with his conviction that the official knew something. He became calm and cool, as was his reaction to danger.

"About two weeks," he answered steadily. "Is he back?"

"He isn't coming back," said Woods quietly. "He's dead."

Gail stared. This must be what was meant by a bombshell exploding in the camp, he thought. Cramer dead? Then he couldn't tell where he had delivered his message! Gail was protected from any possible implication in the Graybolt raid.

"What do you mean, Sheriff?" he asked in a husky voice.

"Just what I said," Woods replied, nodding gravely. "Squirrel Cramer is dead. I received the word late last night. He was shot and killed and his body thrown in a creek down near the town of Graybolt in Wyoming. They found his horse with the saddle marked, also his hat with his mark on it. But they didn't find a thing in his pockets. This was ten or twelve days ago."

"Murdered for his money!" he exclaimed, conscious that both men were regarding him steadily.

"I believe you gave him some," Woods remarked.

"I gave him a roll I had in my pocket." Gail nodded. "I've staked him three times in the last two or three years when I saw him in the southern counties. He had some money from you, too, didn't he?"

"He had some when he started," Woods grunted. "Gail, where did you meet up with Cramer?"

This was the question Gail had expected, dreaded, and was prepared to answer vaguely. If the sheriff had learned this about Cramer, he must also know about Trantler's raid at Graybolt, even though he might not know that Trantler was the leader of the outlaws. Gail looked past the steps at the grass, shrubs, flowers, and trees in the yard. He caught a glimpse of the rich bottom lands through the branches. He envisioned the herds of cattle on the wide range. This was his indirect patrimony from his stepfather, his inheritance from his mother. The picture of Doris Keene, graceful in the saddle, beautiful and dark-eyed, crept in. He would lie, if necessary till doomsday, to protect himself!

"I met him west of Miles City," he said coolly.

"Miles City!" The sheriff pursed his lips as if to whistle, but didn't. Nor did he look squarely at Gail. The latter knew the answer was true, but misleading. It implied he had met Cramer *near* Miles City.

"That's a good bit east of Graybolt," Woods said. "Squirrel would have had to ride some. You didn't meet him in town?"

"No," replied Gail. He had Miles City in mind, thinking

the sheriff was speaking of that town. "He seemed to have a good enough horse, but I didn't expect him to keep along with me . . . didn't want him along. I had too much to think about on the way back for any such company."

"I see," said Sheriff Woods. "I wasn't around when Squirrel started south. What sort of horse was he riding?" The sheriff's gaze was mild as he turned it full on the youth.

"Brown . . . I think," Gail answered with a frown. It was a hard question, because he hadn't seen Cramer's horse. "I'm not sure. I was so excited . . . taken aback by the news he brought me. Say, Sheriff, you don't think *I* killed him, do you?" Gail put the question squarely to forestall others.

"Of course not," Woods said. "But I'm wondering who did."

A wild thought stung Gail as the sheriff spoke. Who *had* killed Cramer? Could it be possible that Cramer's murderer had been one of Trantler's band? Gail didn't dare ask too many questions as to where Cramer's body had been found, but there was another question in his mind that he now put without hesitation.

"Sheriff, how did you know where to send Squirrel Cramer to look for me?"

"I didn't know where to send him, Gail. I asked around and couldn't learn anything, except Stagg said he'd queried the men and a new hand he took on this spring had seen or heard of you down south somewheres. I thought Squirrel could sneak around and find you, and he thought so himself. I knew I could trust him to do his best because there was money in it for him. I reckon he was killed for his money, like you said."

Gail was thinking fast. Stagg had hired a new hand from the south?—a hand who had seen him, knew something of him? This was important, but Gail managed to conceal the excitement he felt inwardly.

"I haven't any idea who could have done it," he said slowly. "He was alone when I met him, alone when he left me . . . or when I left him. I haven't heard a word of him since then till now. If you think there's anything I can do to clear this up, Sheriff, tell me." He spoke in deadly earnest.

Sheriff Woods looked at Griffin and the lawyer shook his head. "Looks like Landon is out of it entirely," Griffin volunteered.

At this moment Gail spied a movement of the green screen of vines at the end of the porch nearest the courtyard. A golden ray of sunlight shot through the leaves for a moment. He rose and sped lightly to the end of the porch, parted the vines, and peered through the aperture. Then he returned to stand by his chair with a thin smile playing on his lips.

"We've had company," he said. "Stagg was back there listening."

"I don't like that," said Griffin with a frown.

"Stagg's been here a long time," the sheriff drawled.

"So long he's forgotten he's working here," said Gail grimly.

"Well, I'm going to scout around an' see if Missus Birch will rustle me a cup of coffee," Woods announced. "You go ahead and do your business with Gail, Frank." He left his chair and went into the house.

"Stagg acting up?" Griffin asked briskly.

Gail told him of the conversation that had taken place between himself and the foreman the night before.

"If that's his attitude, he'll have to go sooner or later," the attorney said when Gail had finished. "You can't afford to have him spread a feeling of discontent and insubordination among the outfit."

"Do you know who this new hand is that said he knew me, or told Stagg he'd seen me down south?" Gail asked casually.

"No. The sheriff talked with Stagg about you. I talked with him about the ranch. You don't know anything more about Cramer than what you told the sheriff, Landon?"

"No," Gail returned coldly. "I wish I knew who killed him."

They talked about the filing of the wills for probate and other matters for nearly half an hour. Then Gail went down the steps and around to the courtyard where he called Stagg. The foreman looked cross as he joined them on the porch.

"I've given Landon the tallies and other sheets and he'll make an inspection of the ranch," Griffin told Stagg. "He naturally wants to check up on the cattle count as is customary in cases like this."

"I ain't got no time to be ridin' around counting stock while the spring roundup's still on," Stagg declared. "Besides. . . ."

"Seems to me that you ought to be out on circle with an eye on the branding instead of hanging around down in the Corner," Gail put in.

"Yeah? So you're gonna teach me my work!" Stagg glanced at Gail, and then turned to Griffin, who had risen from his chair with a serious look on his face. "It don't look good for me, Griffin . . . it's an insult! A recount? Anybody'd think the stock wasn't all here. I don't like it. Looks as if somebody's thinkin' I've been runnin' off cattle!"

"Don't be unreasonable," Griffin said tersely. "You're talking like a schoolboy, Stagg. As an executor of the estate, I'd have to ask Landon to do this even if he objected to it."

"Suppose we wait till after the branding?" Gail suggested.

"It's best to do it at once," Griffin said. "The bank wants its reports over your signature, Landon. Don't forget that like every other rancher you have money borrowed on your stock."

"Huh? He offered to give me my thousand dollar benefit in cash last night," Stagg said derisively.

"You can have that any time you want it," Griffin said irritably.

"And the stock with it," Gail said. "Your hundred head, I mean."

"An' where would I put 'em?" Stagg demanded scornfully. "I'll just take that thousand cash, an' . . . just what's my position on this crazy ranch, anyway?" He glowered at the attorney.

Griffin pressed his lips together, looked at Gail, and nodded slightly.

"What do you want it to be?" Gail asked in a stern voice.

"I want full charge, without any interference, till . . . till you've learned something about the business," Stagg sputtered angrily. "I'm not goin' to move stock, an' count, an' fritter away time on a lot of fool orders given just to see 'em carried out! This ranch is a business, not a game. I know how to run this range an' what's on it without . . . without. . . ." His temper got the best of him, and he swore roundly.

"Without me," Gail supplied icily. "You almost said that last night, Stagg, and this morning you've made it clear. You got sore because I said I wanted the ranch run as Nate Martin would have run it. Well, I still hold to that. I'm here and I'm here to stay, and I'm not going to spend my time sitting on the porch and fanning myself while you tell me what you're doing. You just don't want to get along with

100

me because you don't like the idea of a young fellow owning this property and giving orders. That lets you out!"

"That what . . . *what?*" shouted Stagg in a furious voice.

Sheriff Woods had come to the front door and was standing there.

"You're discharged," Gail said evenly. "Griffin, here, will pay you off on my account. I'm willing to listen to suggestions and take advice, but I'm not going to be talked back to or take orders on my own ranch!"

Stagg's face had gone white; now it darkened with rage. "Why, you young squirt. . . ."

"Enough of that!" Gail interrupted sharply. "I heard you call me that before Luke Denan last night and I won't stand for it again. Take your hand away from that gun or I'll knock you off the porch!"

Gail was as tall as Stagg, not so heavy but more muscular in build. His eyes were flashing dangerously. Stagg's breath was hissing through his teeth, but he hesitated. His hand edged out from his weapon because he had no intention of drawing. Something more than anger glinted in his eyes, for they were gleaming pinpoints of malicious cunning.

"You wouldn't have the guts if the sheriff an' this law shark wasn't here," he gritted. "I'll stay till you've made your count."

"And I'm ordering you to get off my range before sundown!"

"Like hell I will!" sneered Stagg. "I'm still responsible for what's here."

"You'll be responsible *wherever* you are," Gail said sternly. "If you're not clean away from the Hanging X by sunset, I'll have you roped and dragged off!"

"What about the stock I'm entitled to?" Stagg yelled fiercely.

"One hundred head of two-year-old Herefords will be delivered to you at any spot you name within one mile of my range boundary except in the south," Gail answered in an uncompromising voice. "You better get 'em before fall, because I'm not going to feed 'em for you. If you don't want 'em, I'll buy them at the market price and give you cash."

"Borrow it from the bank, I suppose," sneered Stagg.

"Take it easy, Stagg, take it easy," said Sheriff Woods as he came out on the porch. "You've made some strong talk an' Gail has told you where you stand. Looks to me like he's being right fair, an' you're not getting off so bad."

"Do you think he's goin' to run this ranch anywhere except in the ground by turning down me who can help him more than any other man?" Stagg flared in a jeering voice. "What would Nate say?"

"You'd never talk to Nate like you have to him," Woods drawled. "An' you wouldn't spy on Nate by peeking through the vines an' eavesdropping, either. I reckon you better ride on into town with Griffin and me and cool off."

"I'm ridin' out on the range to say so long to the boys," Stagg said narrowly. "Then I'll come in for a settlement with the lawyer."

"I'll ride along with you to see that you don't forget," Gail promised grimly.

Griffin was shaking his head and the sheriff was frowning.

"No, I can't allow that," Woods said. "Part of my job is to scent trouble an' head it off. I'm reading trouble sign here right now. Stagg, you've been ordered off. You're not going to stay here an' make a ruckus. I'm not saying you would, but I'm not taking any chances. Just get together what you want to take along. When I go to town, you're going with me, an' don't make it hard, Jim, because you'll be sorry when you get cooled off."

"You mean to tell me I'm arrested?" Stagg demanded, his eyes glittering through narrowed lids.

"Not yet," the sheriff said sharply. "But you will be if you kick up any fuss."

"I don't want anything like that," Gail put in hastily.

"I'll say you don't!" Stagg cried, whirling on him with an oath.

"It's out of your hands, Gail," Woods said sternly. "And it's out of yours, too, Stagg. I reckon I can find a point in law about this ranch being turned over officially or something like that. The fact is that the new owner of this ranch is here, Stagg. You started something an' it looks like you didn't know where to stop. So I'm stopping it. I'm not going to have any trouble on this ranch, or on this range, nor in this county. That's my say and it goes as put!"

Stagg took a long look at the sheriff. Then he turned on Gail and, to the astonishment of the trio, laughed harshly, but not without a genuine note of merriment. He sobered quickly.

"Listen, kid," he said to Gail, "you'll crawl across the prairie to get me back! I said *crawl*, hear? That's why I'm goin' to humor the sheriff an' take a lay-off." He flashed a dark look at Griffin and strode across the porch and down the steps. "I'll be ready when you are, Woods," he called back.

"A cheap threat!" Griffin snorted. "I pegged him long ago."

But Gail was wondering, and Sheriff Woods was thinking, about Stagg's hints as to Gail's activities in the south. The official was studying Gail's face. He imagined that lines of determination already were beginning to form there. He had anticipated Stagg's attitude, had wondered if Gail would take the easier way and let the foreman ride him. He had no fault to find with the present situation and he wanted to keep an eye on Stagg till the man's anger abated.

"Is there anything more to go over?" Gail asked Griffin.

"The matter of your inventory," Griffin said, "but that won't take long."

When the sheriff had driven away with Griffin in the buckboard and Stagg riding ahead, Gail called Luke Denan.

"Is Chuck Clark still with the outfit?" he asked.

"Shore. Didn't I tell you? Nate's been steppin' him up right along. I'll bet he knows as much about the ranch as Stagg."

"Get that rider you've been holding as a messenger," Gail ordered. "I'm going to send for Chuck."

With this Gail took full charge of his inheritance and invisible trouble clouds rolled and banked and rode in on the four winds to gather above the young owner of the Hanging X and tear the range apart.

Chapter Ten

Chuck Clark had supper with Gail Landon and Mrs. Birch in the dining room of the ranch house. This would have been a signal honor for a hand, but Clark now was range boss, with the authority of a general foreman, under the Hanging X owner. He had convinced Gail of his ability to handle men and his knowledge of the cow business in the hour they had conferred since his arrival from the range.

Gail liked Chuck Clark, who was ten years older than himself. Clark was big and blond, and he reminded Gail of Norm Spencer except that his eyes lacked the flinty hardness of the gunfighter's. Gail was not unmindful that Nate Martin had selected Clark for advancement, and Nate had known men. The young stockman decided that his dead stepfather's judgment was to be relied upon. The two men went out on the porch after the meal. Gail lost no time getting at what was uppermost in his mind now that he had delegated most of Stagg's former duties to Clark.

"The ranch management will adjust itself, Chuck. I'm going to bring a man up from the Flower outfit to help you and me. I met him a couple of times down in the Falls and he knows how to work cows. Stagg said I'd crawl across the prairie to ask him back, but he can't come back here no way an' no how, none! That's flat. I'm going to trust you like sixty because you're honest in mind as well as in eye."

"You can do that," Chuck assured him cheerfully, his

look keen with eagerness. "You've got a big thing here, Gail, an' I want to see you make a go of it. It may sound a little selfish, but I know which side my bread's buttered on, an' you've already boosted my pay. I want to be your top man someday." This pleased Gail and he smiled for the first time that day.

"Let's get away from regular ranch business for a minute," he said. "When I left here, I had a thousand dollars and no more responsibility than a jack rabbit, if as much. I rode a wide trail that narrowed into three or four tight places. A man got me out of those tight places just as I was about to have to use my gun. I thought it was a favor at the time, or until I got to know this man better. Then. . . ." He frowned and nodded significantly. "Not so good," he added.

"An outlaw?" Chuck asked without hesitation.

"One of the worst. I trailed with him a while and I want to blot that out of my life. Today I heard something which has me sitting up an' thinking."

"You heard about the outlaw?" Chuck appeared startled.

"No. He doesn't know what became of me an' I never expect to hear from him or see him again. But, listen, Chuck, Sheriff Woods sent Squirrel Cramer south to try an' find me. He found me and told what had happened up here. I gave him some money an' sent him along before I started up here. Last night the sheriff got word that Cramer had been killed down in Wyoming and robbed."

"By that bandit!" Clark had jumped to the conclusion.

"I don't think so," Gail said. "But he might have been killed by one of the band . . . by one of the desperado's followers. If that was the case, whoever killed Cramer might have learned his mission down there. That's what has me guessing."

"Cramer would be smart enough to talk if it meant saving his life," said Chuck. "But if he thought just his money was in danger, he'd go for his gun. An' he had a stiff right hand. He might have forgot himself an' tried to draw . . . an' caught a slug. Sounds more like it."

This sounded reasonable to Gail, also.

"The sheriff sent Cramer south because Stagg slipped him the tip that a new hand had heard about me, or seen me down there," Gail said earnestly. "Stagg put out feelers after the . . . the accident. Do you know the new men that were taken on this spring, Chuck?"

"Sure," Clark replied. "There were only four who hadn't worked on the ranch before an' three of those come from this north range. There's one . . . a little, dried up, demon of a hoss buster . . . named Beasley, who comes from down Musselshell way. That must be the one Stagg got his information from. Beasley."

"Where is he?" Gail asked with satisfaction.

"He's down in the Corner. Stagg's been grazin' a picked bunch of two-year-olds down there."

"I'll go down there with you in the morning," Gail said. "I'm going to take the stock out of there anyway, but I want a chance to look over this Beasley. They used to call this country up here Trouble Range, Chuck, but if anybody from down below tries to badger me up here, it's going to be that again, only more so!"

Chuck Clark's friendliness, ability, and the spirit of co-operation he manifested renewed Gail's confidence next morning when they rode down to the southeast section of Hanging X range known as the Corner. Here the river badlands bordered on the good grass, with treacherous quicksand "soap holes" covered with a ghostly alkali crust a mere stone's throw away. Nate Martin had regarded the Corner as dangerous and had kept the cattle away from it. Gail already had asked Chuck to move the herd Stagg had been grazing there. He found some four hundred and fifty two-year-olds there, and surmised that the former foreman had intended to select the stock left to him from this herd.

Gail knew one of the hands guarding the stock and spoke to him cordially, receiving a hearty reply. When Clark rode up with Beasley, the new hand from the south, Gail's suspicions were immediately aroused.

"This is Gail Landon, the new owner," Clark introduced curtly.

"Has Stagg quit?" Beasley asked, his beady eyes shifting, roving, staring, spotting Gail from every angle.

"Why do you ask?" Gail demanded. He read in the man's face that he had trailed in hard company.

"I was the last man took on an' I'm hoping to stay on for the season," was the answer. Beasley had betrayed no sign of recognition and Gail could not remember ever having seen him before.

"Are you afraid you won't stay on if Stagg's gone?"

"I dunno." Beasley shrugged his bent shoulders. He gave the impression that he had seen much hard riding, and his general experience bore this out. "He was goin' to put me hoss breakin', but he didn't."

"Clark will give you your orders," said Gail. "Did you tell Stagg you knew me?"

"No, but I told him I'd seen you two years ago when you was in that shootin' contest in Harlowton, an' that I'd seen you early last fall, I thought, down in Livingston. He was tryin' to locate you."

"I see." Gail nodded. He was fairly well known in both places by his real name. The man appeared to be speaking the truth, seemed anxious to keep his job. Also, he seemed to suspect that Stagg was no longer with the outfit. This rider reminded Gail a bit of Squirrel Cramer save that his right hand appeared capable enough.

"What makes you think maybe Stagg has quit?"

"New owners make changes," Beasley replied pointedly.

"You know any reason why he should quit?" Gail asked.

"Sure," was the unexpected answer. "He thought he owned the ranch after the old man got killed." His shrewd eyes didn't blink as he said this.

"Go back to work," Gail ordered, waving him away. When Beasley had left them, Gail spoke to Clark. "Put him with the wagon up above. I want him watched. He's a hard number, Chuck, an' maybe that's why Stagg was keeping him close. I thought Snyder was ranging some Bar Four stuff down here." He was gazing beyond a white post that marked the ranch boundaries.

"Took it out early this morning, I just heard," said Clark.

Gail raised his brows. "That means Snyder got word that Stagg was let out. And Stagg knew I was at the ranch before I sent for him. Looks to me as if Snyder had a spy busy. But I'm just thinking things . . . dreaming. I'll let the facts crop out when they will, but there's something in the wind. How about the cattle count?"

"So far as I know it's all correct," Clark told him. "But we'll check up like you say."

Gail could not shake off the feeling of uneasiness that assailed him whenever he thought of Stagg's threat before he had left. It had not been mere bravado, or plain anger, or over-confidence that had prompted Stagg to say that Gail would crawl to him to give him back his job. Gail began to wonder whether Stagg had not had it in mind to quit in any event and had purposely brought on a clash.

For more than a week Gail was busy on the range, visiting the ranch house only twice in that time. The herds were found intact as reported by Stagg, and indicated by Nate Martin's own tally sheets. There had been a good run of calves with losses infinitesimal. The range was in excellent condition with the mid-June rains improving it. Beef prices were looking up a bit with prosperous indications. Gail felt that with a successful year behind him he would be sitting pretty.

Gail had been up north near the main road for two days when one morning he glimpsed a rider coming from the east. He pushed his horse eastward below the road until he was certain he saw Doris Keene in the saddle. Then he cut around toward Eleven Mile Spring, waving to the girl. She didn't wave back, but she didn't turn back, either. Gail rode on to meet her.

His eyes were sparkling as he galloped into the road beside her. She tossed her head at him with a little smile and drew rein.

"I was hoping you'd ride out this way while I was up here," he told her, fairly breathing in the spirit of wild beauty that she presented with her soft, luminous eyes glowing and questioning.

"I hear you've been keeping awful busy," she said.

"The wind must be able to talk on this range, the way news travels," he said. "I've been taking inventory, as the lawyer calls it. But I was riding over to see you soon . . . honest."

This won a smile. "Father was over to your place the first of the week but you weren't home. He didn't have time to find you on the range. You're invited to our place Sunday for dinner."

"And this is Thursday. Well, I guess I can put in the time till then. Let's ride on to the spring, Doris. It's cool there an' there's shade. It isn't far. I'll race you for it!"

She answered with a laugh and started ahead of him. He kept half a length behind as her splendid mount streaked across the intervening distance. They pulled up in the shade of the cottonwoods, where they could see both ways along the main road and the fork that led down toward the Hanging X ranch house.

"Father told me you fired Stagg," she said, eyeing him closely.

"Griffin and the sheriff were there when I let him go," said Gail with a frown. "They'll tell your dad it had to be done."

"Oh, Father wasn't criticizing. He said you had too much gumption to be dictated to. How are you getting along, Gail?"

"All right so far." Gail was cheerful, frankly admiring. "Anybody asked you to marry 'em since last time I saw you?"

"No." Doris laughed. "Not a soul. You're not hard to tease, Gail. I really didn't expect to see you this morning for I haven't any troubles to tell you. How about yourself . . . all gravy?"

"With sugar on it now that I'm with you," he returned gaily. "Don't elevate your chin, lady, I'm not making love. And I've just thought of some trouble." He nodded gravely.

"There's some trick to this," Doris said with a pretty squint at him. "What is it?"

"I haven't got any slick clothes to wear next Sunday."

The girl laughed and scrutinized him in his blue, soft

shirt, open at the throat, white angora chaps—not exactly needed in hot weather—neat boots, spurred, and wide, gray beaver hat which set off his face and his height. The gun was a necessary implement, and she passed it over.

"You'll do . . . with a necktie," she told him. "Whatever you do, don't drive over in a buckboard or Father will think the ranch has gone to your head." She laughed merrily.

"Now you see," he said in a warning voice. "You're out to make me mad an' I'm telling you that you can't do it." He was forced to laugh with her. "But here's something I better say while I can." He hesitated, then shook his head. "No. I'll leave it till Sunday."

"Can't be so important if it'll keep," she bantered.

Gail had caught sight of a horseman approaching from the west on the road from distant Riverhead. "Here comes a rider," he said, looking about at the paths that led off the road to the sequestered spring. "Let's leave the road, Doris. I'd rather see who's riding this way before he sees us."

"Suspicion or natural caution?" she said artlessly. "Oh, all right, Gail, but I don't care much who sees us. I turn a cold shoulder to range gossip, but then everyone is interested in you. There's no reason why we should be stared at."

They turned off the road into the trees above the spring.

"I reckon we might have been seen the day I came back," Gail said, "because I can't figure how the news got down on the range so quick. Stagg was at the home ranch in no time."

"I told them at home I'd met you," said Doris, "but it didn't spread till next day. Oh. . . ." She raised her brows and stared a few moments. "I saw a hand cutting down behind me as I neared the house that morning. Do you suppose . . . ?"

"Sure," said Gail, nodding his head for emphasis. "Someone saw us. I thought so. Might have been on the look-out for me. And that's just why I want a look at this rider, Doris. I'm going to cut back afoot for a look-see." He dismounted and left his reins dangling as he made his way through the trees to a point where he had an unobstructed view of the road, although he himself was effectively screened from sight by willows.

The lone rider came on at a swinging lope, his hat pulled low to shade his eyes against the dazzling sun. When he reached the spot where the Hanging X road forked off, he pulled up his mount and looked around. His profile, and then the full face, showed plainly.

The world rocked and spun about Gail's head as he recognized the horseman. His hand crossed over to his gun and his face froze into a stern mask that hid his racing thoughts as his eyes steadied. Here was a living, human link between the past and present—a dangerous obstacle looming against the future. Gail's fingers tightened about the butt of his gun. If he had been alone. . . . The rider was Slossom!

Gail breathed the name to himself, but it seemed to his acute senses that the drifting breeze caught it up and shrieked it to the far horizon's rim. From above the spring came the shrill whinny of a horse. The rider looked that way instantly. Gail crept back through the trees, his lips pressed into a fine, white line.

Chapter Eleven

In a natural, leafy arbor beneath the spreading branches of the cottonwoods Gail Landon stopped, stood motionless, struck full tilt by the seriousness of his situation. Slossom at the fork of the Hanging X road could mean but one thing: the outlaw was looking for Gail, who he had known as Lantry. This spot was a long way from the Cutter Ranch west of Libbyville where Spencer had said the raiding band was to meet July 2nd. The date for the rendezvous was less than two weeks away. Slossom would not be riding aimlessly east at this time. The next town was thirty-six miles eastward and there was nothing in it for a man like Slossom. There was no reason to believe that Slossom would quit Trantler and his band unless the outlaw chief were killed and the band broken up, which was improbable. Nor did Gail believe that Slossom could have trailed him even if he had been inclined to do so.

A flashing, kaleidoscopic array of mental pictures and wild conjectures swam before Gail's eyes and set his brain afire. The night Squirrel Cramer had found him in Graybolt—the night of the raid on the Big Horn there— could it be that Slossom had seen the meeting? Could it be that he had met Cramer, forced the truth from him, murdered him afterward? Gail shook his head slowly. This possibility stunned him. But there hadn't been time! He could account for Slossom's movements from before the actual raid until he had fled with the band into the hills. Nevertheless, there was a chance that Slossom had met Cramer when the outlaw was riding to Graybolt before the raid. Gail was conscious of a numbing, bewildering sensation of weakness as he contemplated the chance that Slossom knew his secret. Then his strength returned with a rush, his eyes flashed, his ears became alert. If Slossom were looking for him, he must find him before he could make himself conspicuous by asking questions on the range. But Gail hesitated to show himself because there was the chance that Slossom had left Trantler. Slossom could be on his way to the eastern part of the state or to Canada without knowing anything about Gail's inheritance or his presence in that section.

From the slight elevation where he was standing, Gail could glimpse the dark, cool waters of the spring through leafy apertures and could also see, as through a lattice, short stretches of the road. He remained inactive, indecisive, his ears and eyes alert. Slossom rode into one of the dusty squares of sunlight in the road. He hadn't taken the fork to the Hanging X. His head was up, his hat pushed back from his eyes. Gail knew the outlaw was instinctively wary and suspicious of ambush, and he must have heard the whinny of the horse.

Gail silently withdrew as he saw Slossom turn down to the spring. He now realized that his first move must be to make sure that Slossom didn't see Doris Keene, and the girl mustn't learn anything about the outlaw. Well, here it was—the first bolt out of the blue. He stole back to where Doris was sitting, her horse waiting.

"Why, Gail, what's the matter?" Doris asked as he caught up his bridle reins.

She did not speak loudly and Gail saw that she had read

the signs of his anxiety in his face. He put a finger to his lips as he mounted. There was a trail leading along the bank of a trickle of stream that flowed into the spring, and he pointed to it.

"We'll ride up a ways," he said cautiously. "Walk your horse."

Their mounts made little sound as they followed the soft, grassy trail, and soon they came to a wide coulée, screened by brush, strewn with alders and some wild cherry trees. Here they stopped. They were hidden from view of anyone who might be riding on the prairie, and they were out of sight and hearing from the spring.

"I want to keep an eye on that rider, Doris," Gail said frankly, "and I don't want him to see you, nor me, either, if I can help it."

"You know him?" the girl asked, surveying him closely.

"I think so," he confessed, "and . . . I'm trusting you." He dismounted quickly. "I'm going to take a look-see from the rim of the coulée."

Before she could say anything, he was scrambling up the steep side of the coulée, and, when he could see over the rim across the plain and down their back trail, he centered his gaze on the trees and road near the spring. He could see patches of the road near the spring, but he couldn't see the spring itself. *He might have heard the horses,* he mused to himself, *but he's too cautious to go sneaking along a trail without knowing who he's following. Funny he would hang out in the trees where anybody could pot him.* He remained at his vantage point for what seemed hours, but which really was a matter of ten minutes or so. The presence of the girl below disturbed him.

He looked down into the coulée and saw that Doris had dismounted. She looked up at him and he gestured to her to stay back. When he looked again, he saw her climbing to the rim on the opposite side of the gap in the plain. She did not look across to catch his signal for her to go back down to her horse. As his keen glances swept the road, he saw a spiral of dust to the westward. This was no golden feather such as would trail a horseman pushing his mount in the dust but a swirling cloud such as would be kicked up by a team and buckboard. It was coming too fast for a wagon and soon he descried the dark blot of the horses and vehicle. He looked toward the spring. Would Slossom wait until whoever was coming had passed?

The answer came speedily. Slossom appeared on the road, riding eastward from the spring. He looked back and again his hard features were clearly outlined. Gail could have recognized him easily from that distance even if he hadn't known it was he. Slossom let his horse out and Gail now caught the girl looking in his direction. He signaled to her and went back down the slope.

"You shouldn't have gone up there," he reproved when Doris joined him. "He might have seen you." There was a worried note in his voice that she caught instantly.

"That man is no cowpuncher from around here," she said. "I've seen about all of them, and besides he didn't look like a cowhand."

"How's that?" Gail queried with a frown.

"Too hard and too tough," she replied, looking at him steadily. "Listen, Gail, I'm not a child or a silly schoolgirl. I'm not a meddler, either. But I know you had some wild notions in your head when you left here and that you haven't traveled any soft, straight trail. You went away for adventure and you made enemies getting it. Some of those enemies might follow you up here, and for all I know that rider may be one of them."

Gail stared fixedly at the girl, realizing that this was no idle conjecture on her part. She was talking straight, stating her convictions.

"I'm one who expected you'd have to fight odds to keep what you've got," she continued. "I guess most of the stockmen have a sneaking idea that you'll take the easiest way out and fritter away your property. Don't get angry, Gail. I knew I'd have reason to tell you this sooner or later. I've been keeping an eye out for you and my ears open. I'm not one who thinks you're going to make a bust of things."

"So, you really *did* want to meet me when I came back," said Gail, smiling down at her. "I'm not going to fritter away anything, much less your interest in me, little lady. If there's trouble in the wind, I'm going to shake hands with it before it gets a chance to stab me in the back. I'm asking you to keep all this . . . what has happened this morning . . . to yourself. Will you do that, Doris?"

"I can keep a secret if it's worthwhile," she said seriously. "But that man is riding on toward our ranch." She looked at him as if expecting an explanation.

"I know it," Gail said briskly, "an' that's why I've got to keep an eye on him. I'm going to ride south to where there's cattle an' then cut east to see if he leaves the main road. There's a buckboard coming from town, too." He frowned in thought for a moment. "We better ride down to the road," he decided. "Let's get going, Doris."

They mounted and followed the trail back to the spring. Again on the main road, Gail studied the team approaching from the west. Finally he looked at the girl with a puzzled expression.

"I know that outfit," he declared. "That's the sheriff's team. Maybe he's out with Griffin again to get my reports or with some papers to sign. It means I've got to ride away fast if I'm going to keep track of that fellow an' get to the ranch to see who's coming. The first job is the most important, I reckon. They can send for me from the ranch. They've got all day. An' maybe I'm just guessing. You drift back home easy, Doris, and. . . ."

"If I learn anything out of the way, I'll get word to you," Doris promised, her eyes sparkling. "This takes the edge off of monotonous ranch life, Mister Hanging X, and . . . be careful."

"I'll see you Sunday," he sang as he galloped out of the trees and struck off southeast toward his nearest herd.

Slossom was riding fast on the road eastward as the racing trailer of dust showed. Gail pushed his horse. He wanted to reach the cattle, where his movements would be less conspicuous to Slossom if the outlaw really turned down from the road. If Slossom kept on past the Bar 4, it would indicate he was not headed for the Hanging X, after all. Gail hardly hoped for this. He remembered that the outlaw had stopped at the forks, apparently undecided which road to take. This was no business for a girl to be mixed up in. He kept that telltale feather of flying dust in view as he sped across the level range.

"Good grass, fat cattle, an' a girl to tell my troubles to!" he sang aloud as he rode. "Hello!"

He had reached the van of the herd, but the dust signal had vanished. He strained his eyes, searching for it, and reined his horse to a walk. He believed he could make out the dark dot on the plain, which would be Slossom and his horse. Yes, the dot moved!

Gail halted his horse and rose in the stirrups, his eyes fixed on the blotch in the green sweep of prairie northeastward. Two hours earlier he had been riding, carefree and joyous, to meet Doris Keene; now his eyes were cold and narrowed, his jaw squared, his face stern. The black spot at which he stared constituted a menace and a deadly threat to his peace of mind and the enjoyment of his rightful good fortune, since the latter had to be. Slossom was the link between the reckless and the normal. What . . . ?

Gail looked around. The trees by the spring, the buckboard, the girl no longer were in sight. Gail's gaze flashed back to the dot. He saw very distinctly now that it was moving—moving *southward!* Gail used his spurs and spoke sharply to his horse, and was off at a terrific pace. He swept around the herd and past two cowpunchers standing guard. Then he straightened out for the point where Chuck Clark was superintending the branding.

As the plain literally flowed under his horse's flying hoofs, Gail's resolve tightened. The way to beat trouble was to catch it off its guard. If Slossom was cutting down into Hanging X range because he knew Gail was there, he was acting with supreme confidence, sure that he had the advantage and ready to profit by it.

Chuck Clark rode out to meet Gail when he saw him coming. He appeared startled when he saw the look on Gail's face. Gail's orders were terse.

"Take two men, Chuck, an' ride over east. There's an *hombre* cutting down across our range from the road up above. I spotted him an' I know him. He's bad medicine. Stop him an' bring him to the south camp. Hold him there an' send word to me at the house. Get his gun an' watch him. Make out you think he's a rustler. If he starts anything, you'll have to shoot. I'll be responsible, but don't mention my name. Listen, but don't talk. Go get him like I say. I'm taking Beasley with me to the ranch. Tell the rest of the bunch here to do the best they can till you get back. Tell the men you take with you to do as you say an' keep their mouths shut. I don't think this party will make any trouble. You got it?"

"Straight an' clear," Clark replied. "I'll get the word to you *pronto.*"

Three minutes later Clark and the two others were riding eastward to head off Slossom. Gail and Beasley were galloping for the home ranch. The buckboard was on the Hanging X road and Doris Keene was nearing the Bar 4, having seen the mysterious rider turn south.

Chapter Twelve

Slossom, jogging his horse southward on Hanging X range, made no effort to avoid the three horsemen he saw riding in his direction. Instead, he veered slightly westward and rode to meet them, a move that surprised Clark, who had expected an attempt on his quarry's part to get away. Slossom brought his horse to a halt before the trio reached him. "What ranch is this?" he asked before Clark had a chance to speak.

"You want me to think you don't know where you're ridin'?" Clark retorted. "When did you forget so much?"

Slossom's face froze coldly. "I know where I'm riding. I'm riding to the river ford up here. That wasn't what I asked you." A sharp note came into his voice as he spoke.

"Oh! You're looking for the ford. Well, we're looking for strangers who're looking for fords right now." Clark's tone was icily stern. He whipped out his gun and covered the outlaw in a winking instant.

"Hoist 'em!" he commanded. The two with him also were now bending their guns on the stranger, obeying explicit orders.

"It's that way, eh, cowboy?" Slossom jeered. He smiled evilly, but he raised his hands willingly enough. Clark pushed his horse close and took the outlaw's gun. The two cowpunchers then closed in on either side, putting up their weapons.

"Now you can ride along natural or we'll tie your legs under your horse's belly an' prod you, just as you want," said Clark. "We'll go south toward the ford but we won't cross it. You ready?"

"Sure," jeered Slossom, urging his horse ahead. "I reckon we'll get to see the boss of this outfit sooner or later." He indulged in an ugly laugh.

"You're ridin' with the boss right now," Clark told him. "That's me."

Slossom glanced at him swiftly, his eyes narrowing. "You were lucky to get my gun," he said coldly. "You won't be so lucky at lying."

Clark had seen enough in the other's look and manner to convince him that Slossom was dangerous, tricky, and mean. Gail must have a very good reason for taking up the man, and any reason at all which his owner might have was sufficient for Chuck Clark. He had orders to let the captive talk. Apparently the latter needed but slight encouragement to do this.

"You're no stranger to lying," Clark said loudly. "How'd you get back so quick?" The question was put at random as a feeler.

"I've never. . . ." Slossom checked himself with a dark frown. "Mistook me for somebody else, eh?" he sneered. "You look capable of doin' that."

"The sheriff's better at faces than I am," Clark sang cheerfully.

This brought Slossom's head up with a jerk. What nonsense was this? A sheriff? The outlaw wanted to see no sheriffs! None. Could he have made a mistake? Impossible. He had followed the directions he had obtained in Riverhead to the letter and the landmarks had appeared just as described—the fork of the roads, the spring with its trees, the

123

range beyond for four miles as he had come. He certainly could judge distance. But it bothered him to note that his captor did not look like an ordinary cowpuncher. He could take no chance of a slip-up, not with a sheriff mentioned.

"Do you always talk through your hat when the sun shines?" he asked with another sneer.

"Nope. When I talk with people like you, I don't talk through my hat in any kind of weather because my words might get lost in it."

This and the look that went with it were answer enough for Slossom. He looked straight ahead so his captor could not see the danger lights in his eyes. They were riding at an easy lope now, passing cattle.

"Where we going?" Slossom demanded, unable to keep still.

"If you'll shut up, your mind'll be easier an' you'll find out soon enough," Clark answered sharply. "If you were looking for the ford, it shouldn't matter much. We're ridin' in that general direction."

The outlaw didn't like Clark's tone at all. He cursed himself, inwardly, for having ridden into this hole, for having given up his gun. True, he had another weapon hidden on him, but it would take an appreciable space of time to get it into action. The slowest draw would frustrate the effort. He was not worried save for that sly implication that he might meet up with a sheriff. To determine his next move he had to come out into the open in some measure.

"This is Hanging X range, isn't it?" he asked in a simulated drawl, trying to lift his black brows mildly.

"Thought you didn't know where you were," Clark shot back.

"I didn't say that," Slossom barked. "I said I was riding to the river ford. I know my directions from there to the home ranch house. That's where I was goin'."

"Road was too good for you, that it?" Clark smiled wryly.

"I was takin' a short cut," Slossom snarled. Anger boiled within him as he found himself on the defensive for the first time in years, and with a stranger, too! "This is Hanging X range, all right, an' you better make sure I get to the house. I've got business here."

"Not very much, though . . . here," Clark said grimly. "What name do you use when the sun shines?"

"You're a. . . ." Slossom bit his tongue as he got his rage under control. "I suppose bein' smart is part of your job."

"It's all of it," Clark said with a level look.

Slossom squirmed in a frenzy of fury and recovered with difficulty from this dark mood. To argue with his captor was rank folly and he knew it. Could it be that he was known? He never had been on this range before, although he had heard of the famous brand. But he certainly had heard enough in the darkened rear of the Big Horn resort in Graybolt and had later learned enough from Squirrel Cramer to know that the present owner of the Hanging X would not dare to give him away. The conviction restored his coolness. He jerked his horse to a sudden halt, the others closing in on him instantly. Clark had drawn his gun when he saw the captive's first move.

"There's no use in this nonsense," Slossom said. "If you've mistook me for somebody else, why I'm sport enough to overlook it. I've got business at the ranch an' I can't tell you what it is, but. . . ."

"Shut up!" Clark commanded, growing angry himself. "I'm not goin' to listen to any more of your prattle. Get that straight. The only business you've got now is to mind close that you do what you're told. You're itching to make a false move an' I'll finish it with a slug of hot lead." When he saw Slossom's face turn black with rage and red murder shine in his eyes, Clark spoke to one of the men: "Joe, hop down an' tie him up. Watch out for my gun because I'm goin' to let some of the sunshine he's been spoutin' about through him if he acts queer."

Slossom rose in his stirrups, his hand whipping instinctively to his empty holster like light, his eyes blazing.

"Stop it or take it!" Clark shouted, whirling his horse in front of Slossom's mount and covering him fully with his gun. "Snake him, Joe!" he called to the cowpuncher who already was on the ground with his rope in his hands.

Slossom had to submit. There was no mistaking Clark's look. As his feet were being tied under his horse, Slossom realized for the first time something he had failed to take into consideration. His captor was acting under orders! Then the orders must have come from the ranch owner. The outlaw laughed hoarsely and mirthlessly.

"That's better," Clark said. "Now we'll go along peaceful. If your horse starts to run away with you, we'll rope him, so don't let that bother you. We can be pretty tough with you if you'd rather have it that way."

There was no more talking on the ride to the south camp.

Tied as he was, Slossom had not the slightest chance of escape. Even if he could get away on the horse by some miracle, he doubted if he could release himself. He had to grin and bear it, although, instead of grinning, he ground his teeth to the surging of mad murder in his heart.

Gail saw the buckboard in the courtyard of the ranch buildings when he rode in. The horses had been unhitched and put up. Luke Denan came out of the bunkhouse as

Gail and Beasley dismounted.

"Put the horses in the barn," Gail told Beasley. He turned to Luke. "Who's the visitor?"

"Sheriff Woods is here," Luke said. "I was goin' to send up on the range for you. What do you suppose that law duffer wants?" The old hand's eyes were clouded and anxious.

"More business," Gail returned. "Where is he?"

"Missus Birch called him in to have dinner in the house."

"I'll see him inside, Luke. See that Beasley has something to eat. If a messenger rides in from the range, call me aside. What goes on here isn't any of the sheriff's business at present."

Luke seemed highly satisfied with this and walked to the barn as Gail went into the house.

"Hello, Gail," the sheriff greeted pleasantly. "I didn't drive out here for a good meal exactly, but I wasn't going to turn it down when Missus Birch invited me. Did Luke get you already?"

"No. I rode in without knowing I had company," Gail said, sitting down at the table. He was hungry and set about eating at once. He let the sheriff and the housekeeper do the talking. His thoughts were of Slossom. Now that a link had been established between his newly acquired position and his wild life in the south, he found himself cool, calculating, alert, and exhilarated by the prospect of a fight to hold his own.

After the meal the sheriff accompanied him to the porch. "Have you hired any new men, Gail?" Woods asked when he had lighted a cigar.

"No. I don't need any men at present. Later I may take on an experienced man to help manage the stock."

"Haven't sent for him yet?" Woods drawled, puffing hard.

"No. What are you getting at, Sheriff?" Gail thought he knew and with the sheriff's next remark realized that his surmise was correct.

"There was a feller . . . a stranger . . . drifted into River-head last night an' put an inquiry here an' there as to where the Hanging X was located, who owned it, an' so on. Picked up quite a little information. Word of him got to me, like it would, naturally, him being a stranger an' folks being interested in you. He left town this morning before I got a chance to see him."

Gail nodded and looked coolly at the sheriff. There was no question in Gail's mind but that the stranger had been Slossom. Here was proof that the outlaw hadn't come north by chance. He had come to Riverhead to learn the location of the ranch and to make sure of Gail's right name. He must have had some previous information to send him to Riverhead. Where could he have obtained it? As simple as daylight, this conundrum: From Squirrel Cramer, of course. Then Slossom had murdered Cramer!

"What was his name?" Gail asked complacently.

"I dunno," Woods replied. "He slept in the livery so he didn't have to sign the hotel register an' he didn't tell anybody his name. I heard he was a tough-looking customer. I kept thinking about it till I hitched up an' came out. I thought maybe he might be a troublemaker of some sort, or some kind of an undesirable."

"So you came down here because somebody was asking about the ranch and me, to make sure there was no trouble?" Gail laughed. He was relieved to learn that the sheriff knew as little as he did. At the same time, Woods had imparted some valuable information without being aware of it. "Listen, Sheriff," he said soberly, "men are going to hear about me inheriting this ranch and being a young fellow. They're going to pester me for jobs, I suppose. But nobody is going to make trouble on this ranch if Chuck Clark, my right-hand man, and I can help it . . . which I believe we can."

"You put Clark in Stagg's place?" Woods asked.

"Yes. We've checked up on the cattle count and it's correct. I'll be sending my report to Griffin in a day or two. Where's Stagg?"

"He stayed in town a few days, an' then dropped out of sight. That's another reason why I came over. He made some pretty strong talk to you an' the rest of us. Has he been back here?"

"No, and I don't expect him," Gail answered with a frown.

"I don't know what's come over Stagg," the sheriff pondered. "Old Nate had to keep a tight rein on him, but I reckon he thought he could run you an' the ranch as he pleased. I don't like the way he acted. An' I don't like to think about Cramer being killed. Of course, it happened out of my jurisdiction . . . out of the state, for that matter . . . but I don't like it."

"I don't like it, either," Gail confessed, but this was all he could say.

"I sort of feel responsible," Woods complained. "I sent him down there, but . . . *pshaw!* Squirrel was always making that false pass for his gun an' he likely made it once too many times. He isn't any big loss, being a parasite on society, you might say, but. . . ." He ceased speaking and squinted speculatively at Gail. "You know I believe I've got an idea about who did it," he added.

Gail started and returned the official's gaze sharply.

"Who do you think did it?" he managed to ask in a normal tone.

"I've learned that there was a big raid an' robbery in Graybolt just about the time that Cramer was killed," the sheriff said quietly. "They say that Tarantula outlaw . . . Trantler, he calls himself by rights . . . headed it. I almost think it's safe to figure that Trantler or some of his bunch ran into Squirrel, blotted him out, an' robbed him."

Gail heard this correct theory calmly. He wondered if the sheriff knew more. However, if matters were going to whip to a climax, he was ready for it. Where would the proof come from to link him with Trantler? His eyes narrowed as he thought of Slossom. But if Clark had captured Slossom, he had the outlaw under his thumb.

"That might be," he told the sheriff without batting an eyelash.

"You wouldn't know anything about this Trantler being down there, would you, Gail?" Woods asked in a voice that was almost pleading. "This raid, now . . . there were two men killed in it. It was bold business. Biggest resort in Graybolt. The safe was a bank. Cleaned out. Maybe you heard about it."

"Sure I heard about it," Gail answered readily. "Naturally I knew this Trantler bunch was around somewhere. I got all the underground wires. I didn't say anything. Why should I? With me traveling light, you might say, there's some who'd jump at the chance to think I was mixed up in it. Do you think that, Sheriff?"

The question came sharp and fearlessly, and it apparently startled Woods.

"Why, Gail, I'm not here to think bad of you," the sheriff declared. "The years you were gone are wiped out so far as I'm concerned officially. I'm not thinking anything. I want to see you started right an' I want to see you keep right. That's all."

There was no doubting the sincerity of the sheriff's statement. At the same time Gail discerned that Woods had hoped to obtain some information from him. But Gail was resolved that, if he had to tell his secret to the authorities as a last resort, he would tell Griffin first.

Each seemed to be waiting for the other to speak when a rider galloped up the road from the bottoms. Gail rose from his chair and stepped to the porch rail, where he parted the vines to look into the courtyard.

"Wait till I see who that is, will you, Sheriff?" he said, going down the steps.

"Go ahead!" Woods called after him, knitting his brows.

Gail found it was one of the hands Clark had taken with him. He received the news that Slossom was at the south camp with satisfaction, ordered the hand to hold his tongue, and instructed Luke to see that he was fed and to saddle a horse.

"Tell Beasley I want him to go with me," he added casually.

When he rejoined the sheriff on the porch, Gail was smiling cheerfully. "These are busy days for me, Sheriff," he said pleasantly. "There's a lot of difference between working and. . . ." He caught himself with a grin. "They've got so they send for me when they need me. I've got to go down on the south range. What else you got on your mind?"

"When you coming back?" the sheriff asked.

Gail was disconcerted. The question might mean that Woods contemplated going with him, which wouldn't do at all.

"I'll be close enough to get back before supper," he said.

If the sheriff insisted on accompanying him, he would have to send word to Clark in advance to frame some business down there and to keep quiet about the captive.

"Good," said Woods. "I'll wait for you. Gail, I want to look at your horses in the pasture. I need a good saddle mount an' I'm figuring you're sport enough to sell me one."

"Why, sure," Gail agreed. He speculated as to whether this were an excuse. "Go look 'em over, Sheriff. Take Luke along to show you around. Come and I'll tell him."

They saw Luke leading a saddled horse from the barn for Gail. The old pensioner's wrinkled face wore a worried and puzzled expression.

"I can't find that man Beasley," he told Gail. "He was here a bit ago. His hoss is gone, too. Dropped out of sight just like that." He tried to snap the finger stubs of his left hand.

"Beat it, eh?" Gail was keenly interested. "Did he ask who was in the house?"

"Yes. I told him Sheriff Woods was here. I didn't think that would make any difference."

Gail looked at Woods. "Beasley was the last man Stagg hired this spring. Came from the south, remember? Told Stagg he'd heard of me down there. Looks like he didn't want to meet up with any sheriffs."

Woods remembered very well, remembered more than he had told Gail. He merely nodded and stroked his mustache. "Maybe it's just as well," he said. "I wouldn't bother about it. You're not short-handed."

"Luke, the sheriff wants to look over the horses in the pasture," Gail said briskly. "You take him down. Maybe he'll want to buy one, so be careful what you show him." He laughed as he mounted swiftly.

The cheerful, carefree look on Gail's face froze into stern

lines as he galloped away from the ranch house. He had intended to take Beasley with him and permit the man to see Slossom, thinking he might recognize the outlaw and show it in some way, or say so in as many words. Now there was no doubt but that Beasley had been riding a rough trail in the past. Hadn't he fled at the prospect of meeting a sheriff? He had pay coming to him, too. But Gail doubted that he would return to get his money. What concerned Gail most was the fact that Stagg had hired Beasley. There was some connection there. More links? With the sheriff suspicious!

"Matters sure are tying themselves up into knots," he told his horse as he rode, "but I'm going to untie one of 'em this afternoon!"

The south camp was a cabin and corrals near some hay sheds in the bottoms. The cabin was occupied in winter at times when the men had to feed the cattle hay. Gail found Clark waiting for him in pleased anticipation.

"He's inside," Clark said when Gail had dismounted. "Didn't offer no resistance, you might say. Had to tie him on his horse when he started to argue. He looks bad enough to me. He knew this was Hangin' X range, all right. I don't believe he saw the brand on the cattle we passed because I kept far enough away from 'em. Said he was looking for the river ford, an' then that he was heading for the home ranch on business. Didn't mention your name, nor did I. He's tied up in there an' mad enough to fight a bull bare-handed."

"Good," said Gail grimly. "He's an outlaw up here to try to blackmail me, Chuck. That's my guess. The sheriff's up at the house. He heard about this *hombre* asking about the ranch an' me in town. I don't want the sheriff to know he's here, not yet, anyway. Beasley beat it when he learned the law was on the ranch. Think that over. I'm going inside. Come a-running like a monkey, if I whistle."

Chapter Thirteen

Gail stepped into the cabin, flooded by sunshine streaming through three windows, and found Slossom lying on a bunk, bound hand and foot. He looked at Slossom quizzically as the outlaw recognized him and tried to rise.

"Hello, Slossom," Gail greeted cheerfully enough. "What're you doing here?"

"Lantry!" Slossom exclaimed hoarsely. "Take off these ropes that fool thought he had to use. Hurry up!"

"Oh, call me by my right name," Gail said easily, taking out tobacco and papers. "You know what it is." He tapped the tobacco from the muslin sack into a paper and eyed the outlaw.

"You don't want to be called by the old name here, eh?" Slossom sneered. "Oh, you needn't be afraid of me. I'll forget it except when there's nobody around to hear."

"The real *old* name is my right name," said Gail, fashioning his cigarette in skilled fingers. "I've used Lantry now and then, but at present I'm using my real name. Let's hear you say it." He snapped a match into flame and lit his cigarette.

"Landon, then," Slossom growled. "Wanted to find out if I knew it, did you? Well, you've heard me say it. Get these ropes off me, Landon!"

"I was aware that you knew my right name," Gail said, pulling out a chair and sitting on it with its back in front of him. "You inquired in town about my name to make sure, and you asked the location of the ranch. If you were coming here to see me, why didn't you take the road up there at the forks by the spring? Didn't want to attract attention? Well, you probably wouldn't have been grabbed and roped if you had come in the proper way." He blew a perfect smoke ring nonchalantly. A faint smile played on his lips.

"You know a lot," the outlaw scoffed. "Well, so do I. Did you order that range rube to drag me in this way?" His words bristled with menace.

"This isn't welcome range for strangers," Gail evaded. "You must have looked suspicious. The man who brought you in isn't such a rube as you think. I notice he got you dead to rights." The smile broadened.

"Because I let him, you fool!" Slossom blurted angrily. "Do you think I'd have let him draw down on me if I hadn't known where I was an' what I was about?"

"What were you about?" Gail asked, a frown chasing the smile.

"I came here to see you," Slossom barked. "That ought to be enough. I can talk better when you jerk these ropes off."

"Oh, you're doing pretty well. How'd you know I was here?"

"I trailed you, of course. You didn't think I was going to take a chance on you yelping, did you?"

"You'll have to tell me a better one than that, Slossom," Gail said coldly. "Are you sure you didn't know who I was and where I was from before you left Graybolt that night? You know the night I mean."

"What if I did?" Slossom flared. "I did you a good turn, if I knew, didn't I?"

"How was that?" Gail asked, appearing surprised.

135

"By sending you with your pal Spencer up on the divide next morning so you could make your getaway," Slossom answered heatedly.

"Oh! So that's how it was. Did you tell the chief what you knew so you could frame it for me to slope?"

"You know better than that, Lantry . . . Landon, I mean. I fixed it so you could get away, an' I came up here to see how much you appreciate it."

"So you did know about me before the raid," Gail said, his eyes narrowing. "You've just the same as admitted it."

"What if I did," Slossom repeated. "I did you a favor, didn't I?"

"You didn't do me any favor by killing Squirrel Cramer," Gail shot back sternly.

Slossom stared at him. Surprise, conjecture, speculation were commingled in his gaze, which kindled into a look of dark cunning.

"He double-crossed you an' then drew down on me," he said.

Gail's lips curled. "You admit that, too . . . the killing! Cramer couldn't draw down on you. He had a stiff right hand . . . been that way for years. He probably told you something to save his own life and you shot him down like a dog and robbed him! You'd do a thing like that, Slossom."

"You didn't think you was runnin' with angels when you was trailin' with Trantler, did you?" Slossom sneered. "Any of your friends around here would laugh at you if you told 'em that. But they wouldn't laugh if they knew you was in that raid down there an' had killed a man yourself!"

His harsh laugh of scorn brought the white into Gail's face. "Well, you're not going to get the chance to tell them," he said grimly. "Let's hear what you wanted to see me about."

"Loosen these top ropes so I can sit up," Slossom growled. "I can talk better that way. Oh, you needn't be scared. They took my gun an' my hands are tied anyway." He didn't look so fierce as he made his request.

Gail whistled shrilly, and Chuck Clark was in the cabin in a moment.

"This *hombre* says he can talk better if we take the ropes off his chest and midriff so he can sit up," Gail told Clark. "He also called you a range rube, Chuck. It's up to you."

"If I had my way about it, I'd set him loose so he could try to back that up," Clark said. He laughed at Slossom. "You don't look as smart as you look mean. What'd you call me that for?"

"Lemme up!" Slossom roared as he twisted in a super struggle to loosen the ropes.

"Let him sit up, Chuck," Gail said. "I want to hear what he has to say."

"Sure." Chuck laughed. He unfastened the ropes that bound Slossom to the bunk. "There you are, Snake Eye . . . all set to speak your piece."

"Sit down, Chuck," Gail invited, motioning to a chair.

"You don't want him here," Slossom said quickly.

"Why not?" Gail countered. "He's a good listener."

"Then *I* don't want him here!" Slossom exploded. "What I've got to say has to be said to you alone. You ought to know that."

Gail signaled Clark to leave. "Got to humor him," he explained.

"You're not sittin' as pretty as you think, Lant . . . Landon," Slossom hissed through his teeth, his eyes flaming, when Clark had gone. "That was a rough game you were in down below."

"Is that a threat?" Gail asked narrowly.

"It's a reminder." Slossom managed to swing around to the edge of the bunk. "I'm not here to make trouble for you, but I figure you owe me something for. . . ." He paused with a heavy scowl.

"For helping me get away?" Gail asked pleasantly. "Why, Norm Spencer might have shot me."

"He didn't, though. I knew he wouldn't an' so did you. I got you away, all right. Now, isn't it worth anything to you to be away . . . to be back an' safe? It won't take me long to clear out an' never come back. The game I was in is gettin' too hot, anyway."

"What do you want?" Gail asked curiously.

"Now that's something like it," Slossom said eagerly, his eyes sparking. "We'll say I learned something from Cramer." He paused with a cruel grin. "You never could prove I killed Cramer," he said confidently. "But let's say I knew you had a lot at stake. This is a fine big ranch . . . worth more'n half a million, they tell me. I knew Trantler had took a liking to you because you was so fast with your gun. He intended to keep you with him till the next job. Don't think I don't know what I'm talkin' about. I know. I helped you to get away. We were chased an' lost a man. It might have been me. I've quit the gang. I thought you'd appreciate what I've done. I'm headed for Canada. It's worth ten thousand dollars to you, at least . . . an' you're done with it." He smiled in triumph, so he thought.

"How many stock ranches do you think have ten thousand cash at this time of year?" Gail inquired.

"You've got it," Slossom declared with conviction. "An' if you haven't that much, you can get it easy enough."

"And how much will Trantler have when he comes?" Gail asked.

"He won't come. Do you think I'd be a fool to tell him

an' let him double-cross me?"

"Sounds reasonable, Slossom . . . if the lie didn't show in your eyes," Gail said coldly. "Now, you listen to something. How could you prove I was ever with the gang? Who'd take your word after they found out who you were? Especially when you killed Cramer? Would Trantler be ready to tell anyone, and would *his* word be taken? Do you think any of those other cut-throats would come forward and tell?" Gail laughed derisively. But he sobered when he saw the gleam in the other's eyes.

"There's one who will be tickled to death to identify you!" Slossom cried hoarsely. Then he lowered his voice. "Jordan, the look-out, wasn't killed! You hit him, but not so bad . . . just hard enough to knock him down an' send him to a doctor to have the bullet pulled out. He's around an' he saw you. I know because I've been in Graybolt since the raid!"

There was a truthful ring in his voice that impressed Gail despite himself.

"Now, think!" Slossom hissed. "Do you remember when you untied the knot an' took that handkerchief off yourself? Remember where it was? It was the first time you'd ever wore a mask, wasn't it? You bet it was. An' in your excitement *you pulled it down!* I saw you when you busted out the back door an' the handkerchief was hangin' on your neck like a scarf! Your face was uncovered. Jordan saw you in the lamplight plain as day. He could pick you out of a million!"

"If I thought you were telling the truth, you'd be taking an awful chance, Slossom," Gail said slowly.

"Why?" The question came like the crack of a whiplash.

"Because I could have you put away," Gail answered grimly.

"Kill me off?" sneered Slossom. "Too many questions,

boy. Besides, I may have protected myself against you gettin' away clean."

"You talk like a schoolboy!" Gail ejaculated. "This was a poor time to visit me, Slossom. The sheriff of the county heard about you asking questions in Riverhead last night and he drove out here this morning. Maybe you saw the dust from his buckboard behind you? He's up at the ranch house now."

Slossom's jaw dropped, then clamped shut as he stared. But what Gail had said had made its impression. "It won't get you anywhere to cook up something like that."

Gail smiled. "I see you've got to know all of it to be convinced, Slossom. I happened to be up by Eleven Mile Spring when you rode in from the west this morning. I watched you. You stopped where the road forked off to the southeast toward the Hanging X. My horse whinnied. You looked around quick. Then you rode on to the spring and watered your horse. You saw the team and buckboard coming from the west and decided to ride on ahead of it and cut down across the range, instead of taking the road where you might be seen. You didn't see any sign of the buckboard when you turned south, did you? Of course not. What you told my man Clark about looking for the river ford was as big a bluff as you are. I had dinner at the house with my friend, the sheriff."

"Then why didn't you turn me over to him?" Slossom challenged.

Gail didn't answer this. Instead, he whistled again for Clark. When Clark entered, Gail pointed to Slossom. "Search him," he directed.

"Like hell!" shouted Slossom, lunging toward Gail, his tied hands upflung.

Clark caught him and threw him back on the bunk. "Not

so fast, Snake Eye," he cautioned.

"That's right," Gail said quickly, "just hold him and I'll do the searching myself."

Slossom let out a string of horrible oaths while Gail speedily went through his pockets, removing their contents and felt him over.

"I thought so," he said as he brought out the hidden gun. "And look here, Chuck! . . . he's got two watches!"

"Sit still now," Clark told the outlaw. "Sit still or I'll forget your hands are tied and knock you cold."

Gail was examining one of the watches that was a thick, heavy silver timepiece of the old school. "There's a mark scratched in the case of this one," he said to Slossom. "Funny." He glanced at Clark. "It's Squirrel Cramer's watch," he said wryly. "Look at it, Chuck, and don't forget that our friend here was packing it."

Slossom's face was livid, his eyes blazing balls of fire.

"I reckon they'd believe me now," Gail told him sternly.

"I never saw that watch before!" Slossom cried hoarsely. "He sneaked it out of his own pocket!"

"I told you that you wasn't smart," said Clark. "I was watching. You don't think I'm a *blind* range rube, do you?"

Slossom twisted in a frenzy of rage, choking out oaths. At this moment a whistle sounded outside. Clark stepped to the door, looked out as a voice came to him. He whirled with changed expression.

"Woods is riding in with Luke!" he exclaimed.

"The sheriff!" Gail leaped from his chair.

"Keep him out if you can. He mustn't know this fellow is here."

As Clark left, Gail looked about the cabin swiftly. "There's no place to hide you, Slossom," he said guardedly. "The bunks are too low, an' . . . I'm going to take a chance

141

an' untie you, so the sheriff won't get wise."

He lost no time in liberating the outlaw.

"If you try a trick, I'll stop you with a bullet!" he promised, and Slossom knew he meant it. "Were you going to beat it to the Cutter Ranch at Libbyville?"

Gail asked this hoping to confirm the rendezvous that Spencer had told him was set for July 2nd. As he waited for Slossom's reply, he scooped up the watches, money, and other articles he had taken from the outlaw's pockets and thrust them into his own. Hoofs were pounding outside.

"No, I. . . ." Slossom caught himself with an oath, and Gail turned to look at him sharply. Slossom's hesitation, however, had informed him of what he had wanted to know. "I told you where I was going," the outlaw hissed. "You better be careful. Lant . . . Landon!"

A horse loomed close to the door, partly shutting out the light. Gail took two steps toward the door. Then he whirled, remembering the weapon he had taken away from the captive. But Slossom had moved with the speed of a panther. The table was bare. Slossom had secured his gun!

Chapter Fourteen

Slossom sat down on the edge of the bunk, his right fingers under his coat, as Gail looked at him narrowly.

"You're goin' to be right or wrong, for once in your life!" Slossom said significantly, his beetling eyes giving his words their potent meaning.

"I can beat you to the draw, Slossom," Gail said. "Remember that before you try anything. Your name's French. You came here looking for work, that's all. Stick to it if the sheriff talks to you. Maybe he knows who you are already, but if he does, I didn't tell him. You're in a tight corner and I'll shoot your tongue out before I'll let you talk!"

Clark entered the cabin and the sheriff's voice sounded.

"Get over at the window, Clark," Gail told him quickly. "Watch French . . . that's his name . . . he's got. . . ."

Slossom's sudden roar of laughter drowned Gail's words and before Gail could speak again the sheriff was at the door.

"Well, here you are, Gail. I picked a horse in the south pasture straight off an' we rode along the bottoms to see the hay. It looks good. Reckon you remember how I used to come out every spring an' look around the ranch with Nate. I sort of feel at home here, boy."

He took off his hat and mopped his brow as Gail said something pleasant.

"It's getting powerful hot," Woods continued. "I'll just

come inside a minute. Good thing we've had our June rains, boy, or this heat would dry up the cricks an' springs six weeks ahead of time, to say nothing of the oats. An' they talk of growing wheat here! One blast of the hot winds an' the crop would shrivel."

Gail had no alternative but to invite Woods inside. He never had heard the sheriff so voluble, and wondered at it.

"Hello," Woods greeted Clark. He shot a keen glance at Slossom and nodded. "Am I interrupting business down here?"

"Not very much," Clark answered with a look at Gail. "We're about through branding an' was figuring on another hay shed." This was an excuse which Woods could fathom as he pleased. The sheriff paid no attention to it.

As Woods sat down in a chair, Slossom's darting glances settled on him and caught the gleam of his badge peeping from beneath the left side of his coat. But the outlaw required no flash of a badge to convince him when he saw a sheriff. He had spotted Will Woods as one the first moment he set eyes on him. What kind of a play was this? Had Gail—Lantry, as he knew him—tattled? When he looked swiftly at Gail and caught a warning in the youth's eyes, he scowled in uncertainty. He was not left long in doubt as to the sheriff's presence.

"New hand?" Woods asked Gail with a nod at Slossom. He took out a cigar.

"Stopped on his way north to ask for a job," Gail answered. "What do you think about my building another hay shed, Sheriff?"

"*Humph.*" Woods bit off the end of his cigar, thrust it into his mouth without lighting it. "Nate always managed," he said. He was looking straight at Slossom.

"Where from?" he asked genially.

"Musselshell," Slossom told him.

Gail's ears pricked up because this was the country that Beasley had claimed to hail from, and Beasley had been careful to avoid meeting the sheriff. It was getting so that incidents seemed to fit together like cogs in a wheel.

"Little late in the season to be lookin' for a job," the sheriff observed.

Woods's tone convinced Gail that the official had headed for the south camp purposely. Could Woods know anything about Slossom? What the outlaw had said to the effect that Gail had pulled down his mask during the raid on the Big Horn resort down in Graybolt worried Gail. To save his life Gail could not recall if his mask had been tightly about his face under his eyes when had been forced to shoot the look-out, Jordan. He hardly remembered untying the knotted handkerchief. If he hadn't killed the look-out, he was glad of the fact, but danger lurked in Jordan's recovery if what Slossom had said was true. He could not help but doubt that Slossom had been back to Graybolt. But the outlaw might easily enough have had word from there. Unlike Trantler, who was a tyrant—mean, vicious, uncouth, evil, and domineering, but clever at outlawry— Slossom was of a sneaking breed: sly, snaky, sharp, cunning to some extent, but possessed of a hot temper. He might backtrack to Graybolt with a posse searching and get away with it.

"I wasn't looking for a job till I crossed the river an' saw this ranch," Slossom said, trying to smile agreeably with the result that his lips twisted unpleasantly. "This looked like a good berth till winter." Good enough explanation for any sheriff who didn't know him.

"Oh, did you ride down the river from town?" Woods inquired.

"From what town?" Slossom demanded crossly.

"From Riverhead. You was there last night, wasn't you?"

Slossom jumped to the conclusion that the sheriff had seen him. Clark thought the same thing and was much interested. Gail was sure the sheriff had secured a good description of the stranger he had heard about and was assuming Slossom to be that man. The situation was becoming ticklish.

"Why all these questions?" Slossom demanded in a surly tone.

"Oh, don't get huffy," soothed the sheriff. "A man in my job is always interested in strangers. Some bad ones come through up here, an' . . . well, all of 'em don't get clear through. It's right in my line to look a stranger over. I see your holster is empty. A good sign?"

Gail shot a swift glance at Clark, who was looking at Slossom's empty holster. When Clark gazed in his direction, Gail, who was standing to the left and a step behind the sheriff's chair, tried to signal him that Slossom had the second gun. He didn't know whether Clark understood the gesture or not and he could not continue without attracting the attention of both the outlaw and the sheriff. Gail had not really had time to draw down on Slossom and disarm him before the sheriff came to the door, and he had not wished to precipitate a gun play. Now he looked steadily at Slossom and rested his hand on his weapon. Slossom, in possession of his gun, was dynamite; and Gail was not going to take a chance, since the responsibility was his.

"You don't wear a gun when asking for a job?" the sheriff was saying. "That's funny, too. Most riders pack one, 'specially when they're traveling cross-country. Horse might throw 'em and drag 'em or something."

"No horse throws me," Slossom bragged insolently.

"Slick rider, eh? Well, you ought to find it easy to find a job. Haven't you got a place for him, Gail?"

"Not at present," Gail replied, directing a double meaning at the man on the bunk. He detested having to play a part. "He might try the Bar Four."

Sheriff Woods shook his head. "Keene's got more men than he needs, so he says. Maybe this fellow better ride back to town with me an' make a few inquiries there."

Slossom laughed. "You make a business of gettin' strangers jobs besides askin' 'em questions?" he sneered.

"If they want them an' can show me they're entitled to them," the sheriff answered sharply. "I don't think you want any job." His voice changed with this and he leveled a cold gaze on Slossom.

"That's what these boys think," Slossom retorted defiantly.

"It's like this, Sheriff," Gail put in desperately, "this man came riding along our range and Clark brought him here to see me. I haven't got anything for him." It was keeping within the truth. Before he could continue, Slossom rose from the bunk, speaking briskly.

"Seeing as how there's nothing here for me, I'll be riding on." He took one step toward the door that Gail blocked, when the sheriff stopped him.

"Sit down!" Woods commanded. "I'm not through with you."

Slossom's eyes narrowed and snapped. "You tell him, Lantry," he said to Gail threateningly.

"The name's Landon," the sheriff interposed. "But he's through with you. It's me who's dealing with you now. Sit down while I tell you why I'm asking you questions."

Clark had moved toward Slossom. The outlaw sat down with a snarling oath, his beady eyes fixed on Gail. The latter was frowning. Slossom could have carried the acting off better than he had. He had no business showing antagonism toward the sheriff, and his tongue was too sharp. It was a bad situation with Slossom in possession of a gun. The outlaw held his right hand in his lap so the fingers were just inside his coat. Gail knew he had the gun in his waistband where he could draw with a snap of the wrist—a dead shot, to put it bluntly and accurately.

"I'm asking all strangers who come up from Musselshell way or any other place south where they've been lately an' what they were doin'," the sheriff said sternly. "Can you answer that?"

"Sure," Slossom snapped. "I been in Lewistown lately an' gambling for a living. I haven't got a cent left . . . not even my watch. If you don't believe me, you can search my pockets. I lost everything. That's why I was thinkin' about a job. Here!"

Almost before they realized what he was doing, he stood up and turned his pockets inside out, one by one, disclosing the soiled linings.

"Cleaned out," he said, sitting down. "I even lost my gun!"

Woods appeared taken aback by this. Gail looked at Clark with a grim smile, but Clark was grinning at what he thought was extreme cleverness on Slossom's part. Slossom looked as if he had been mistreated and was appealing for sympathy. But his right hand was again in place for a sure-fire draw.

"Did you only have one gun?" Gail asked pointedly to attract Slossom's attention and in an effort indirectly to warn the sheriff. Gail's hand was resting on his own weapon.

"I reckon I wouldn't need but one here," Slossom flashed back.

"Why talk about guns?" Woods drawled. "There was a robbery down in Graybolt a while back. You been down in Wyoming?" He leaned a little toward Slossom, searching the man's eyes for a true answer.

"Oh, that's it!" Slossom exclaimed. "You got me pegged for a bandit? If you have, you're sure on a cold trail. Snowed over. No, I ain't been down in Wyoming."

But the sheriff had seen a spark in the man's eyes. "Where was you playin' in Lewistown?" he demanded.

"Every place where they had cards," Slossom answered belligerently. "Name any place an' I've been there." His gaze shot past Gail to where he could see a horse in the shade of a tree near the cabin.

"I see," the sheriff said slowly. "Ever visit a place called the Big Horn?"

Even Gail was startled at the sharp tone in which the sheriff thrust the name of the resort at Slossom. The outlaw noticed Gail's start and the look in his eyes and mistook it for something else. His face went black with rage.

"You ain't said nothing, you double-crosser?" he shot at Gail.

"You're stepping into the fire, you fool!" Gail retorted hotly.

"Answer my question!" the sheriff thundered.

"Why don't you ask Lantry . . . that's the name *I* call him!" Slossom cried. "Ask him where he's been!"

Gail's face went white under its tan. He could see that the outlaw thought he had told the sheriff about him, thought he had sent for the official, perhaps. There was also the chance the sheriff already knew! It was this last which stayed Gail's impulse to draw.

Unexpectedly the sheriff rose suddenly from his chair. In doing so he stepped directly in front of Gail. There was a brief moment in which Slossom's mind sensed instantly his opportunity to make a break.

Gail's warning cry came instinctively with the outlaw's decision. Gail literally flung the sheriff aside as Slossom leaped from the bunk, his right hand snapping forth with a glint of steel and a blazing bullet. The shot missed Gail but left the breath of the bullet in his face. The outlaw plunged through the open door as Gail fired from his hip.

Clark's jump for Slossom had brought him up against the table that the sheriff shoved forward in steadying himself. Clark was around it in a bound, leaping with Gail for the door. The sheriff roared an order that none heard, and lunged ahead of Clark, blocking the door.

A bullet shaved splinters from the doorjamb as Gail rushed outside. Slossom had almost reached the saddled horse under the tree. His left hand was outstretched to catch the reins. He whirled, and his gun came up as Gail dashed toward him, his weapon glinting steel-blue in the sun. "Drop it, Slossom!" Gail commanded hoarsely.

Slossom's eyes were blood-red balls of fire, blazing with fury as he heard Gail call him by that forbidden name.

Then came the fleeting, instantaneous look which gunmen sense rather than see in the wink before the draw or shot. In this brief flicker of time a thundering report came from the doorway of the cabin.

Slossom stumbled, firing aimlessly into space as he fell forward on his face and sprawled with arms outflung, clutching at the grass, his fingers gradually relaxing.

Gail turned to see Sheriff Woods, standing tall and straight, a smoking six-shooter in his hand, white lines creasing his weather-beaten face, and Chuck Clark peering from behind him. Gail walked, white and straight-lipped, to the sheriff.

"Why did you do it?" he asked in a hard, firm voice.

"Because he would have killed you," the sheriff snapped out.

"Are you sure that's what you think?" Gail demanded.

But Woods pushed past him impatiently, putting up his gun.

Luke Denan had come on the run from nearby. He rolled the still form over on its back and felt inside the damp shirt. As the sheriff came up, and Clark hurried toward them anxiously, leaving Gail alone in the blazing sun, old Luke withdrew his hand that was warm and red.

"Must have split his heart," he said, looking up in awe. "He's . . . dead."

Gail heard and stepped grimly into the cabin—to think.

Chapter Fifteen

Gail Landon stood by the table in the center of the cabin and stared out the window at the hayfield and the trees beyond. His sense of security in his new rôle as a ranch owner was disrupted. Slossom had told him just enough to make him uneasy. If Jordan, the look-out, had been but slightly injured and if Gail had indeed pulled down his mask during the raid in Graybolt, then he could be positively identified and picked out as a member of the notorious Trantler band. Word of Slossom's death would spread and carry by little known channels to the ears of Trantler. The arch outlaw might not attempt to avenge his lieutenant's death if merely the sheriff were concerned. But if he learned—or knew— about Gail, he would act. This seemed certain. With everything at stake, Gail realized fully that he must act first.

Why had the sheriff been so quick to shoot? To assume the responsibility, of course. It was the sheriff's idea, then, to protect Gail? Did he know more than Gail suspected and did he propose to shield him? Gail scorned this possibility. He had stepped into the dangerous adventure with Trantler with his eyes open. It was up to him to get out of it, not by circumventing the law or lying, or hiding behind the sheriff's authority, but by foiling Trantler.

Gail's mind was made up within two minutes. Gradually, as his face set sternly, he became aware of the brilliant green outside the window. But a brown splotch of color seemed moving among the trees beyond the field. A horse? Perhaps a horse and rider. But there were no riders in the bottoms; no stock except in the pastures. The spot of color vanished. But Gail could not shake off a vague feeling that he was being watched. Then he remembered Beasley. Perhaps the new hand was waiting until the sheriff left to report back. But this was but one of many riddles.

When Sheriff Woods again entered the cabin, he stopped short, struck by the cold, grave expression on Gail's face.

"I told Luke and one of the hands what to do," he said. "I'll have to bring the coroner down in the morning, I reckon. I shall have to explain that I wanted this man, that he was picked up on the ranch acting queer, an' that he started a gun play which I finished. I'll fix it so you'll be in the background. So you needn't worry."

"Are you doing all this to shield me . . . to protect me?" Gail asked spiritedly. "You know very well that I knew that man."

"Of course, I do," Woods said impatiently. "An' I can hear, can't I . . . an' I can see a gun when it's under my nose, or your nose, can't I? I knew that fellow was no good an' here for no good purpose the minute I set eyes on him. Do you think I want the word to go out that you were in a shootin' match on this ranch already?"

Gail's face had paled, but his resolve to settle his own troubles in his own way was unshaken.

"I can't blame you, I guess," he said finally, "but. . . ."

"I should say you can't blame me," the sheriff interrupted, "an' I don't want to hear any more about it. What do you know about him?"

"I was up north this morning. Rode over as far as Eleven Mile Spring. I saw this fellow riding east and I recognized him. I saw the dust your team was kicking up and then

153

made out the buckboard. I rode back, keeping an eye out, and I saw this man cut down on my range. I sent Chuck to pick him up and bring him here. Then I hurried up to the ranch to see you, because I suspected it was your buckboard I'd seen on the road."

"Why didn't you tell me this at first?" Woods asked quietly.

"Because I wasn't sure that man had come up here looking for me."

"Plausible," said the sheriff, with a frown, "but not enough. After you found out he was looking for you, then what? He didn't ride here without anything on him. He gave the liveryman a ten dollar note from a roll, I heard. Oh, he's the stranger who was in town last night, all right. He spent money there, too. And he wore a gun. I saw through his play about having lost everything at cards. The lie was in his eyes. Now what did he have in his pockets?"

Gail smiled grimly. Here was a showdown he had to meet and he was ready. His answer was to take the money and other articles that had belonged to Slossom from his pockets and put them on the table—all except Squirrel Cramer's watch. He kept his left hand closed on that in the left side pocket of his trousers.

The sheriff made a hasty examination. "What about the gun?" he asked, looking up suddenly.

"Chuck took a gun from his holster when he stopped him. He had a second gun hidden on him."

"You didn't find it when you searched him?" Woods arched his eyes in surprise. "You didn't find it an' give it back to him, did you?" he asked suspiciously when no answer was forthcoming.

"Hardly," said Gail dryly. He was thinking about this.

"You sure he didn't have anything else on him?" the

sheriff persisted, looking at Gail steadily.

Gail drew the watch from his pocket and handed it to him.

Woods took it with a puzzled air, examined it, opened the case at the back. Then he started and stared hard at Gail. "Squirrel Cramer's watch!" he exclaimed. "He had this on him?"

"Yes. Clark was in here when I searched him and he saw me take the watch off him. It explains how he got up here. He met Cramer, got some information from him some way, shot him, and robbed him. He came up here thinking he could blackmail me. That's the water in the bucket . . . *all* of it, Sheriff."

"You called this fellow Slossom," said Woods slowly. "Was he running with Trantler down there?"

Gail's face might have been chiseled out of marble, so stolid was his expression. He returned the sheriff's look coldly. "I've answered all the questions," he said, his lips hardly moving, "and I have no more information." There was a note of finality in his voice.

"I suppose you know that I'm disposed to be your friend?" Woods said significantly.

"I'll try to protect the both of us," Gail said simply.

"You better go see Griffin when you're in town again," Woods said. He gathered up the things on the table and put them in his pocket as Gail stepped to the door. "You may need me yet!"

If Gail heard, he paid no heed to this. He went out to find Clark alone. He walked straight to him with a question in his eyes.

"Luke an' Joe took it away," Clark told him.

"Don't give out any particulars about this to anyone, Chuck," Gail told him. "Does Joe understand that, too?

Good. No one can get anything out of old Luke. Chuck, Beasley beat it when he heard the sheriff was here. Sneaked his horse out of the barn and sloped. He may report back after Woods goes. If he comes to the house, I'll probably send him back to the wagon. If he reports to you, I want to see him. I thought I saw a horse in the trees on the other side of the field. I wish you'd take a look over there and see if you can spot anybody or catch sight of any sign that anybody has been around. I told Woods about searching that fellow and gave him what we found, including Cramer's watch. I suppose he'll want to talk to me some more but I haven't anything more to tell him."

Gail had spoken crisply and to the point, and had held Clark's attention closely. Clark noted that a change had come over Gail.

"I'll ride around over there for an hour or two," he said.

"Go ahead," Gail told him, "and report to me at the house later."

He watched Clark mount and ride around the end of the field.

The sheriff came out of the cabin. "I guess I'll drift along," he said. "I want to get back to town by dark."

They rode on to the house without saying a word. Gail was waiting for the sheriff to open up again, but the official was uncommunicative. When they reached the house, Woods asked that his team be hitched to the buckboard. Gail told Joe and the other hand there to wait until Clark showed up. He kept reasonably close to the sheriff until the latter was ready to leave. Before Woods got into the buckboard, he turned to Gail.

"I'm not asking you to talk if you don't want to," he said, "but don't get caught up on anything later."

Gail watched him drive away, wondering if this were advice or a threat. He dismissed it as a formal warning. He would not so have dismissed it if he could have seen the deep lines of thought in the sheriff's face, his frown, alertness of eye, and heard the remarks he made to himself as he drove along the dusty road.

Clark rode in late in the afternoon. He had seen nothing, had no news.

"Very well," Gail said. "Take Beasley back on and watch him if he comes back. I'm going away on a little trip. I'll be gone several days. I'm leaving you in charge of the ranch. If you're not quite sure about anything, Luke might be able to help you, or there's Griffin, my lawyer, in town. Part of your job is to see that nobody gets on this ranch who doesn't belong here, and, if they do get on, you're to see that they get off."

"That's an order," Clark said. "I got it straight." He would have liked to ask Gail some questions, but Gail's look stopped him. He rode away with Joe and the other hand who had been with him to return to the scene of the branding. Luke was to keep an eye on the house and the bottoms.

After supper Gail ordered a horse saddled. He told Luke and Mrs. Birch no more than he had told Clark. He rode away with a small pack on the rear of his saddle within half an hour.

The road was a gray ribbon of dust flung northward among waves of green prairie in which there were golden ripples where the grass was turning in the heat. A rosy glow bathed the open land in soft color. The buttes to eastward were pink in the sunset's reflected afterglow. Crimson banners streamed above the western mountains. A hundred miles to the north the three purple peaks of the Sweetgrass

157

Hills floated dimly in a sea of blue.

Gail shook out his reins and breathed deeply with the wind in his face. As he rode, he shook off the weight of his worry. He was, for the time being, on the adventure trail again and his blood leaped at the thought. This time he was not riding aimlessly, ready to grasp at the first straw of excitement; he had a definite purpose—a goal. He proposed to beat the news of Slossom's death to Trantler's rendezvous! He was going to Libbyville, and, if necessary, to the Cutter Ranch, and he intended to reach there before the day set for the gathering of the band. There was not time to ride a horse that distance and reach there the week before the projected meeting. So Gail would take railway trains to the nearest point from which he could ride to Libbyville. First he must see Norm Spencer. It was Spencer who had seen him first when he had rushed out the rear of the Big Horn after the raid. Spencer had been with the horses and had called to him at once. Spencer would know positively whether or not he had been unmasked. Gail hoped to learn if Trantler shared Slossom's secret.

Although Gail was not riding his best horse, as he would have to leave his mount at the railroad point on the High Line, he made good time. The dark shadow of the trees at Eleven Mile Spring speedily came into view. Gail was riding fast to put the main road behind him. He could catch a train at midnight bound west to Shelby. There he would change for a southbound train, and in the southern part of the state he again would change west to the town closest to Libbyville.

"Hop to it, hoss!" he sang cheerfully. "Old man time's ridin' ahead of us an' we got to catch him!"

He passed the spring with the first blue veils of the twilight drifting across the land. Open prairie now—straight north. The Sweetgrass Hills were cloaked in haze and the red in the high skies had died to a silvery sheen. But Gail had his landmarks—the little creek, coulées, a trail of low buttes—to guide him. The little town on the railroad he was heading for was the shipping point for that range.

He looked back and brought his mount to a halt. His brow wrinkled into a frown. A blue of shadow was moving on the golden ribbon that was the main road, east of the spring. He had seen no rider, but that flying dot certainly *was* a rider! Could Doris Keene have been at the spring? Well, someone had been there and had seen him!

Gail rode on, convinced that he had been watched from the day of his first arrival on Hanging X range, and he was convinced, also, that this riddle would solve itself—with his help. He smiled grimly. It was all up to him and he was glad of it. The shadows came marching down and a first brave star hung like a lighted lantern, harbinger of the night. The breeze freshened as the black velvet curtain spread over the sky and gleamed with festoons of stars in which a silver crescent of moon sailed majestically.

Gail reached the town on the railroad shortly before midnight. He put up his horse at the livery with instructions to the livery man to look after it until he returned. He saw no one he knew and boarded the westbound train. He rode on trains the rest of the night, the next day, and most of the next night, till he alighted in the early morning at a town twenty miles north of Libbyville.

He refreshed himself with a few hours of sleep and a hearty meal, and early in the afternoon hired a horse and set out southward across a rolling country bordering on a range of timbered hills.

Chapter Sixteen

Libbyville drew business from several quarters. Cattle, sheep, farming, and mining contributed to its seasonable prosperity. It derived some profit, also, from an itinerant minority of its population which patronized its score of gambling and drinking resorts when out to celebrate. It was close enough to the hills to attract a bold, lawless element that preserved it as something of a sanctuary.

Gail rode slowly from the railroad point and reached the town just after sunset. He put up his horse and went to a small café on the main street for his supper. The brim of his hat was drawn low, but his gaze was alert below it for glimpses of any of Trantler's followers. In the time he had spent with the band he had learned that it was the outlaw leader's custom to have been looking over the ground in advance of a raid. Since a big 4th of July celebration was scheduled in Libbyville, he had little doubt but that Trantler had a resort or bank here spotted for looting. To the best of Gail's lean knowledge, Slossom had been the advance man in the past, with Spencer and another helping him. At Graybolt, Gail had been in the town with Spencer before the raid as a part of his training. Gail expected to find Spencer this night. If he wasn't in town, Gail proposed to inquire casually about the location of the Cutter Ranch and look for him there. It was only a short time before the 2nd of July.

It was dark when Gail, having sauntered up and down the main street, turned into a resort blazing with light, noisy with the uproar of a boisterous crowd, and showing other indubitable signs of being one of the most popular places in town. He threaded his way through the jam of spectators about the gaming tables, scanned the faces he could see at the bar, and was brought up with a start as he felt a firm grip on his right arm. When he looked around, he found himself staring at Norm Spencer. His eyes lighted with pleasure.

"This is luck!" he ejaculated, and would have held out his hand had not Spencer kept hold of his arm.

"No heroics," Spencer said in an undertone that Gail didn't like. Spencer released his grip on Gail's arm. "Let's go back," he said, leading the way by a tortuous detour to the rear of the big room. They went into a passageway and entered a private card room.

Spencer lighted a lamp on the table, and closed the door. Gail had noted a lack of cordiality in his former companion's manner. Now he found himself on his guard as he met Spencer's cold scrutiny.

"When did you get in?" Spencer asked.

"Two hours ago. I didn't expect to find you this quick."

"Oh! You was looking for me?" Spencer's lip curled slightly.

"Why not?" Gail demanded. "Is there anything wrong in that?"

"Maybe so, maybe not. I suppose you thought the chief would be tickled stiff to see you after the way you lit out, an' what happened afterward." Spencer's tone came near being a sneer.

For one brief moment Gail wondered if the news of Slossom's death had already reached Trantler's ears, but this seemed impossible, and Gail dismissed it.

"I didn't expect he'd be tickled by my leaving as I did," said Gail, "but what do you mean by what happened afterward?"

"We were chased an' almost cornered an' lost a man." Spencer never once took his eyes off Gail's.

"What's that got to do with me?" Gail flared. "I couldn't have done much if I'd been along."

"Slossom took after you an' said you rode back toward Graybolt," came the answer. "He hinted you might have tipped off the posse to cover yourself up. I caught hell an' smoking brimstone. Trantler nearly drew down on me. I told 'em your horse stumbled into the shale an' that I shot three times as a signal. The chief had to believe me or try to kill me. I've got a lot to thank you for!"

"You may have before I get through," Gail said evenly. "I took a chance on losing my horse and maybe breaking my neck getting away. An' I didn't ride east. I rode north. An' I didn't see anything of Slossom or of any posse. Now tell me I'm lying!"

Spencer looked at him closely and appeared doubtful.

"You've got nerve to come here, anyway," he said, frowning. "The chief will probably shoot you on sight."

"Then I better see him first," said Gail grimly. "Is he here?"

Gail's manner and the tone of his voice took Spencer aback.

"Listen, Norm," continued Gail, lifting his brows with inspiration; "if the chief thought I was dead wrong, why didn't he change the place where the gang was to meet? Wouldn't he think I'd give it away?"

This was a poser and Spencer could think of no quick answer.

"You know better than to think I'd talk," Gail said coldly.

"We split up when we was chased," Spencer growled. "We only got part of the divvy. We had to work so fast the chief didn't have time to tell us to meet at a different place, or he didn't think of it."

"Has he or any of the men showed up yet?" Gail asked.

"Some of the men are around, keeping low," Spencer replied. "I expected Slossom before this." His look did not encourage frankness on Gail's part.

"Do you think I've lied to you?" Gail asked sharply.

"I don't know what to think!" Spencer declared narrowly.

"Then I'll give you something to think about," said Gail. "An' I'll tell you not to fly off the handle with me unless you mean it!"

"Tough as cactus, eh?"

Gail ignored this. "I'm going to tell you why I had to leave the morning after the raid," he said soberly. "A messenger found me by accident in Graybolt and brought the news that my mother and stepfather had been killed in an accident. I had to get home."

Spencer saw the naked truth in Gail's eyes. "You went straight home?" he asked in a changed voice.

"Yes . . . and that's all of that, for the present."

"I reckon I've got to believe you," Spencer decided aloud. "I thought probably it was a girl. You could have told me."

"No, I couldn't. You remember I went out of the Big Horn when we were keeping watch there before the raid? Well, that's when I went looking to see if the messenger had left town. He had given me the message in the back room, just before. If he had found me a day sooner, I wouldn't have been in the raid."

163

"Don't know as I blame you," Spencer grumbled. "But I wouldn't have said anything if you'd told me."

"There was a reason you'll maybe learn later, Norm."

"You were afraid to trust me," Spencer accused.

"Put yourself in my place and remember I'm trusting you now."

Spencer looked at him curiously. "Say, listen, Lantry, you've got something big on your mind. Come on an' let's have it."

Gail looked at the door. "Think we're all right here?"

"Sure," Spencer answered, also nodding. He sat down in a chair and took a pack of cards from his pocket. He began shuffling them. "If anybody busts in, we're playin' a private stake till a game's ready."

Gail sat down near him and lowered his voice. "I've got to know if Trantler's here," he said.

"Not yet," Spencer told him with a puzzled frown. "Slossom has to get here first."

Gail leaned close to the other's ear. "Slossom isn't coming," he said softly. "That's why I wondered if Trantler had shown up."

Spencer stopped shuffling. "Ain't coming? Why not?"

"He's dead," Gail whispered. "Killed day before yesterday."

Spencer leaned back, staring hard. "How . . . why . . . are you sure?"

"Dead sure, Norm. He tried a gun play and a sheriff shot him up in Montana. Now here's a coincidence. Listen! The man who brought me the message that my mother and stepfather had been killed in an accident was waylaid right after he left Graybolt . . . about an hour before the raid, I figure . . . and murdered and robbed. Slossom did it. He got some information from the messenger before he killed him and followed me up north after he left Trantler. He got caught up there and the messenger's watch was found on him for proof. He was going to blackmail me because he thought that I had inherited a lot of money. That's how he came to send you and me up on the divide together the morning after the raid. He knew I would make a break for it and he knew you'd let me get away. He wanted me to get away instead of staying a long time, maybe, with the chief. And I'm not sure he didn't tell Trantler what he knew."

"Are you sure you didn't kill Slossom yourself?"

"Sheriff Will Woods up there killed him as you can easy enough find out. If he hadn't, I would have had to do it myself."

Spencer pursed his lips and squinted in thought.

"Trantler wouldn't pull this raid without Slossom, Norm. Not in this tough town. And Trantler isn't here. Maybe he's up north, too. How many of the men are here?"

"Half a dozen," Spencer growled, his eyes narrowing. "An' they're the poorest in the bunch so far as brains are concerned."

"Trantler isn't going to show up!" Gail declared. "He's left the rest of you to hold the sack!"

"Hold on a minute," Spencer cautioned. "You're losing your stirrups ridin' this wild story so hard. What do you mean . . . we're holding the sack?"

"You'll be holding it yourself if Trantler doesn't show up," said Gail soberly. "Here it is three days before the Second . . . the day the outfit was to congregate. It'll be two days tomorrow. An' Trantler hasn't showed up an' Slossom isn't coming. Did you ever know the chief to be this late?"

"No," Spencer confessed uneasily. "I've been wondering a bit. Do you know where he is?"

"Not for sure, but I've got an idea he's up north . . . a

long way from here. Slossom was killed day before yesterday. I came most of the way here by train. I wanted to see if Trantler was here, but I also wanted to see you. There's something weighty I've got to ask you."

"Shoot!" Spencer invited with another dark scowl.

"Think back and think hard," said Gail earnestly. "After the Graybolt raid, when you were on your horse an' holding mine, waiting, I was the last to come out, remember? You called to me. Was I masked when you first saw me? Was the handkerchief over my face, Norm? Think hard."

"No, it wasn't," Spencer answered readily. "How do you think I spotted you so quick? Why, what's up?" He was frankly puzzled.

Gail was sitting, tight-lipped, his face pale, his eyes flickering with sparks of green fire. Slossom had told the truth! He leaned toward Spencer again, smiling faintly.

"There's a lot to this," he said. "I met Slossom and talked with him before he ran into the sheriff. He told me he had doubled back to Graybolt, had learned that I hadn't killed that look-out, Jordan, and that I had pulled down my mask in the excitement. He said Jordan was just wounded and that he would know me if he ever saw me again, and could identify me." Gail waited for this to sink in. "Then he asked me for ten thousand dollars . . . which I didn't have . . . to keep his mouth shut!"

"He probably lied," Spencer said slowly. "It sounds like a fairy tale."

"He might not have doubled clear back there, but he might have heard something," Gail pointed out. "He was Trantler's scout, wasn't he? He had ways of getting information, didn't he?"

"What would make him think you had ten thousand dollars?" Spencer asked curiously. Then his expression changed quickly. "You say you talked with him an' I reckon you did. I'm taking what you say for the truth because I don't see where it would get you anything to be making this all up. I can't say as I'd blame you a bit for popping Slossom over to protect yourself. Did you do it?"

Gail shook his head. "I told you the sheriff got him."

"I reckon you better tell me what you're keeping back," Spencer said soberly. "You've got me walkin' up a ladder with my feet between the rungs."

But Gail's head was up and he was slowly and silently getting to his feet, his eyes fixed on the door. Spencer shot a glance at the door just as the knob turned and it opened a few inches. Gail leaped to it and flung it wide.

A huge bearded member of Trantler's band stood in the doorway, his eyes sparking jet. Crowding behind him were five others who belonged to the band. The leader pushed into the room with the others following.

"What do you want, Miller?" Spencer asked the leader.

"I saw you sneaking back here with this fellow an' we thought we'd ask what was up," Miller said in a deep, guttural voice with a leer at Gail. "What's he back for?" There were murmurs from the others.

"Because he's reporting," Spencer snapped out. "An' it's nothing to bother you."

"Oh, ain't it? Well, it bothers us just the same. We don't like the way things are shapin' up. Slossom ain't here, an' the chief ain't here, an' now this Lantry shows up. Next thing we know the law will be down on us like a mountain tipping over. What's he reportin'?"

"Reporting business," Spencer shot back. "Don't forget I'm in charge here till the chief comes. I'll tell you what it's all about out at the ranch later. It doesn't look good for us all to be making a jam back here. It'll attract attention."

The men with Miller were muttering and scowling heavily.

"It don't look good for you two to be back here framing up anything, either!" Miller exclaimed angrily. "We heard this Lantry was dirt, an' now you're catering to him!"

"That's a lie!" cried Gail scornfully. "Get that out of your head."

"Shut up!" Miller roared. "Another peep outta your mug an' I'll cuff you through the window!" His eyes were blazing.

"Not so loud," warned Spencer, holding up a hand. "Miller, what're you tryin' to do? . . . start trouble right here in town ahead of the big play an' crumb it?"

"Rats!" sneered Miller. "There ain't goin' to be no big play, an' you know it! If a raid's comin' off, tell us where Slossom is! Tell us why the chief ain't here. Tell us where the rest of the gang is at! Two of the boys just came in from the ranch an' there's nobody there but old Cutter. An' he ain't heard a word. But you know something, an' this runaway squirt isn't here for his health. You don't have to sneak off an' put your heads together to ditch us, an' you ain't goin' to get away with it!"

Both Spencer and Gail realized that Miller and his companions meant trouble and plenty of it. Gail sensed an opportunity to get Spencer away from the band and was ready to welcome it. At the same time he was ready to fight with his hands or his gun at the first sign of actual hostilities. The outlaws were rough and capable in their way, but they were not quick or clear-headed. Trantler had not left them behind for nothing, and he had left Spencer in the cold because Spencer had been friendly with Gail. It was as clear as sunshine.

"Get out of here!" Spencer ordered. "We'll talk this over

at the ranch. There'll be a bunch breezin' back here in a minute."

"You're tellin' us to get out, eh?" Miller looked at the hard faces about him. "Hear that, boys? Wants us to get out so the two of 'em can sneak for it." He glared at Spencer. "If you're in charge, why don't we crack this joint? There's money here enough for the few of us."

"There's a go," said one of the men with Miller.

"What about it?" said another. "We're ready."

"You've been drinking," Spencer charged. He lowered his voice. "The big loot won't be here till the Fourth. We can't just walk in on 'em without any plan."

"You don't want to walk in on 'em," sneered Miller. "You don't figure to do nothin' a-tall. You an' that wine-sap. . . ."

"What's going on in here?" came an authoritative voice from the passageway outside the door.

In a wink Gail leaned over and blew out the light in the lamp. He leaped aside as a red tongue of flame stabbed the darkness and the room rocked to the thunder of a gun.

Chapter Seventeen

In the brief interval that followed the blowing out of the light and Miller's shot, three moves were made simultaneously in that darkened room. The air swished with the swing of a chair as one of Miller's companions hurled it through the window, smashing sash and panes and letting in a rush of breeze and an eerie glow from an alley. Men jammed the window, struggling through it to escape. Gail leaped around the table toward Spencer as the room shook again to the roar of guns. A bullet fanned Gail's cheek as he fired at the flame blazing almost in his face. Miller's huge dark form crashed down against the table, sending it to the floor in a pile of kindling.

"The door!" Gail cried in Spencer's ear. "We'll go out the back!"

The faint light from a bracket lamp in the passageway outside illuminated the doorway and spread into the room like a pale mist.

"Take the window!" Spencer commanded, holding Gail back and thrusting his gun out the door to shoot.

The lamp was shattered and rained glass and flaming oil to the floor of the passageway, almost in the faces of men who were crowding in from the main room of the resort. As Spencer stepped back, Gail slammed the door shut and snapped the catch on the lock. Spencer was at the window and Gail stumbled after him. In a breath of time they were in the open air.

"Don't follow the rest of 'em!" Gail said hoarsely. "This way, Spence!"

Shouts and the splintering of wood sounded through the window as the door was smashed in. Behind the resort was a fence, its boards ghostly gray in the starlight, with dark shadows of trees beyond. Gail fairly dragged Spencer to the fence, and they climbed over it, dropping into a yard behind a house. "Those fools will run to the street an' start the whole town after 'em!" Spencer panted, breathing inarticulate expletives.

"What do you expect?" Gail said crisply. "Trantler wouldn't have ditched 'em if they'd been smart. Without him controlling 'em, they'll run straight into hot trouble."

"Miller won't lead 'em!" Spencer ejaculated grimly. "I got him. He wanted to kill the two of us."

As they slipped through the shadows to a back street, Gail wondered which of them had shot the outlaw rebel. It didn't matter. "We've got to slope out of here *pronto*," he told his companion. "This thing coming off just ahead of the celebration will stir up a hornet's nest in town, an' bullets sting like sixty when they come from live guns. I reckon I got you into this business by showing up like I did, Spence, an' I'll take you out of it. The livery's on this street. Is your horse there?"

"Sure it's there," Spencer growled. "The rest of 'em leave their nags tied anywhere. Let's get goin' while the crowd's still millin' around that joint tryin' to find out what it's all about!"

They got their horses and rode quietly out of town, avoiding the main thoroughfare. When they broke through the trees with the shadowy plain before them, Gail spurted into the lead and turned north toward the town on the distant railroad where he had obtained his mount. They rode hard for a time, and then swung east to the road, where they eased their pace.

The night sky was splashed with stars under the high-riding crescent moon. The horses' hoofs beat dully in the cushion of fine dust. The air was balmy and sweet-scented. It was like riding forth into a new world after the violence in town.

"Trantler ditched you because you were friendly with me," Gail told Spencer. "I'll make you see that before daylight comes."

"He didn't show up an' he didn't send no word," said Spencer. "That's enough for me. Even if he was afraid to tackle the raid with Slossom gone, he could have sent me word. I always thought there was a rat winking in his eyes. Now I know it!"

Gail said nothing for a time as they rode along the gray ribbon of road. The fact that Trantler was not at the place of rendezvous convinced him that the outlaw had shared Slossom's knowledge gained from Cramer. Whether he had others of his band with him or not, Gail believed Trantler had been working with Slossom in some way. By this time he might know of Slossom's death. He would suspect Gail and then—would he raid Hanging X range? Had this been the plan all along?

Gail drew a long breath and called a halt. He looked into Norm Spencer's brooding eyes and spoke rapidly in a cool, firm voice.

"Spence, I was left a big ranch up north by my mother. That's why Slossom thought he could blackmail me. He thought I'd pay big before I'd take a chance on letting it get out up there that I'd been mixed up with outlaws. I think Trantler was to show up later and get his . . . if he could.

Slossom's gone and I won't give in to Trantler, not an inch. If this hadn't happened to me, I would probably have kept on the wild trail for a while. But I was getting sick of it. I reckon you're getting sick of it, too. You've told me enough while I've been with you that I'm sure you know cattle and how to work them. I've got a place for you up there on the ranch if you want to come along. Think it over while we're riding to town."

He spurred his horse lightly, and they rode on. This time it was Spencer who was doing the hard thinking.

"Looks to me like there might be some trouble up your way," Spencer said to Gail some time later.

"They used to call it Trouble Range up there, years ago," Gail responded.

Spencer said nothing for more than an hour, and finally the lights of the town glimmered like fireflies on the shadowy swell of the plain. The horses broke into a ringing gallop, sensing warm quarters, feed, and water ahead. Gail sang a snatch of a cowboy song. He knew he was taking a chance with Spencer, but it did not worry him.

"If there's going to be more trouble, I want it all in a bunch," he told his companion cheerfully. "I'd rather take it coming than have it chase me going. Figure that one out!"

In their accommodations in a rooming house near the livery an hour later, Gail talked slowly in a low voice while Spencer listened, smoking innumerable cigarettes. Gail was cleaning and oiling his gun as he carefully explained his situation.

When he had finished, Spencer looked at him quizzically, but not unfriendly.

"You know I'm a pretty tough egg," Spencer said. "I won't chase dogies for forty a month an' found. If you took me on your payroll, you wouldn't be hiring just a ropin' hand, nor a waddie to stand guard on a wet night, nor a horse wrangler." He looked at Gail steadily. "Do you get what I mean, Landon?"

"I do," answered Gail evenly. "I wouldn't hire you as a common hand."

Spencer lifted his brows. "You want to hire my gun, too?"

"I do . . . if I need it . . . and if your brains go with it," Gail answered soberly.

"Well, then, I guess I'm tied up with a cow outfit," said Spencer in a tone of resignation. "But suppose this sheriff of yours gets to askin' *me* questions?" he blurted with a frown.

"I'll leave it to you to answer them," Gail said with a laugh.

"An' suppose he doesn't like my answers . . . then what?"

"That'll probably bother him," Gail drawled, yawning. He drew off his boots, unbuckled his gun belt, and hung it from a bedpost. "You'll have to leave your horse here to be pastured out. It would take us too long to ride to the ranch. We're taking a train at six in the morning, so we better grab a couple hours of sleep."

"A train!" Spencer exclaimed. "I'm gettin' civilized again!"

At daylight on the second morning after their flight from Libbyville they reached the railroad town on the High Line. After a hearty breakfast they went to the livery where Gail got his horse, which he had left there, and secured a temporary mount for Spencer. They left town immediately and swept southward across the rolling prairie on their way to the ranch.

Gail was glad to have Spencer along. Their closer association during the long, hot ride on the train had convinced him he could trust this companion of his wild adventures. Gail's thoughts kept time with the beating of his horse's hoofs. He had learned what he had set out to ascertain. Trantler had ignored the rendezvous. Gail had been *unmasked* at the end of the Graybolt raid. He now knew just where he stood, and the knowledge strengthened his determination to thwart any attempt on the part of Trantler or anyone else to take advantage of his past dereliction.

As they rode swiftly in the keen morning air, he described the lay of the land to Spencer.

"You stand to be a pretty big bug up here, don't you, Landon?" Spencer bantered. "I feel tempted to hold on an' cinch a permanent bunk with you . . . at good pay." His eyes sparkled with the challenge.

"You've got the chance, Norm," Gail sang cheerfully.

When the trees about the spring came into view, he searched the plain and the ribbons of road with an alert gaze. He caught his breath and his eyes narrowed when he saw a feather of dust curling on the west road signaling the approach of a rider from the direction of Riverhead.

He called sharply to Spencer, and they pulled up their horses.

"See those trees down ahead of us?" he said, pointing. "Well, that's the location of Eleven Mile Spring that I've told you about. I have reason to think I've been spied on every time I've been there since I've been back. But the days of spies on the Hanging X are over. There's a rider coming on that road over west." He pointed to the moving dust spiral. "That horseman may be a stranger, or a 'puncher from some other ranch . . . or somebody else. But we're going to beat him to the spring to make sure he

175

isn't on the look-out for me!"

With this, he spurred his horse and they raced for the trees. Before they reached the fork of the road, Gail had recognized the man in the saddle on the oncoming horse.

"It's my former foreman, Jim Stagg," he announced grimly. "I told you about him. I said if there was going to be more trouble, I wanted it all in a bunch. Maybe it's going to start."

"An' when it's starting is the best time to stop it," Spencer told him as they spurred their horses to head off Stagg.

Chapter Eighteen

Stagg brought his horse to a rearing halt amid shooting sprays of dust at the crossroads and waved a hand to Gail as the latter rode up with Spencer.

"Was down at the ranch yesterday an' day before an' they said you was away, Gail," he hailed, looking keenly at Gail's companion.

Spencer returned the scrutiny with a cool gaze.

"What were you there for?" Gail asked sharply.

"Oh . . . business," Stagg answered. He nodded toward Spencer. "New hand?" he inquired blandly.

"Might be a friend visiting me," Gail returned with a frown. "You can speak up about your business, Stagg."

The ex-foreman's eyes flashed. "I reckon I better see you alone," he said in a tone that lent significance to his words. "I've been on a little trip myself. This is sort of . . . er . . . private."

Gail didn't like this, for he caught a glint of dark cunning in Stagg's eyes and the subtle hint of patronage still was in the other's voice.

"Concerns the cattle you have coming, I suppose," he conjectured.

"Oh, I'll take those down in the Corner tomorrow or next day, maybe," Stagg said carelessly with a disparaging gesture. "No, I. . . ."

"Now, just a minute," Gail interrupted sharply. "I'm not

delivering any cattle to you in the Corner or anywhere else on my range. I told you I'd deliver the hundred head of two-year-olds to you a mile off my range, except in the south. I won't deliver in the south because the badlands are there. I don't reckon Keene wants you to take 'em on his range, which bounds mine on the east. This leaves you the west and north to choose from. One mile in either direction. Say where and I'll deliver 'em. That fixes that."

"Yeah?" Stagg's eyes narrowed. "You said once you'd give me beef steers instead of two-year-olds. Remember that?"

"Sure. That was before you flew off the handle entirely."

"Then you said later that you'd buy 'em from me an' give me the cash," Stagg said harshly.

"You turned that offer down, too. I'm not buying any stock."

Stagg's face darkened. "Those answers are straight between the eyes, all right," he ground out between his teeth. "Looks to me like your word ain't worth much."

"I've got an answer for that, too, Stagg. I'll give you ten days to take delivery of your cattle so you won't have any excuse for ridin' to the ranch to see me. If you want cash for the stock, you can deal with somebody else. 'Most any stockman would make you a fair offer. As for me, I've got more stock than cash."

"I guess you could spare a hundred dollars a head for my lot," Stagg sneered.

"And make you a fat present above market price?" Gail said angrily. "You haven't got that fool idea of making trouble out of your head yet, have you, Stagg? Well, this spot is just off my range. Why not start it here an' now?"

Gail slid out of his saddle with the last word and beckoned to Stagg from the ground.

"Get down here!" he challenged. "Get down an' toss your gun aside an' I'll knock the fool notions out of your head with my fists!" His own weapon leaped into his hand and he put it down in the grass, stepping away from it.

Stagg's face was nearly black from frustrated rage. Gail's action had caught him by surprise. He glared at Gail in indecision, but he certainly had no intention of fighting the youthful ranch owner with his hands.

"You better hear what I've got to tell you in private before you go flyin' off the handle yourself," he said harshly.

A cool laugh came from Spencer. Gail picked up his gun instantly as Stagg looked at Spencer savagely. Before Stagg could speak again, Gail was in the saddle, motioning to Spencer.

"Ride along down that road toward the ranch, Spence, while I hear what this *hombre* has to say. He says it's private, which shows that he's afraid to talk in front of people. That means it's dirt. If I don't like it, I'll make him repeat it in public!"

Spencer's laugh came again as he turned his horse down the road.

"You've imported a gunman!" Stagg exclaimed when Spencer was out of hearing.

"I reckon you're forgetting that I'm a gunman myself," Gail shot at him. "If guns was all I had to think about, I could depend upon my own alone."

"You said something," Stagg sneered. "You remember I said I was on a little trip? Well, I rode down south a ways. I heard things. You wasn't so smart to get mixed up in that Graybolt raid with Trantler. Now your eyes start to open. It's different when you find out I know something, eh? You killed Squirrel Cramer yourself so he couldn't tell where he found you an' what he knew. An' this feller who got plugged on your ranch the other day knew too much, too! You'd plug *me* this minute if you thought you could get away with it! But you can't pour soft soap over everything. Now, do you think those two-year-olds are worth a hundred apiece?" He closed in a hoarse voice of triumph.

Gail's lids had narrowed to slits. "I'm just thinking how blamed easy it would be to frame you, Stagg," he purred. "Why, it'd be so easy I don't see why I don't do it. All I've got to do is make you draw an' shoot you off your horse. The sheriff an' others know you tried to start trouble at the ranch. I could say you came out an' started trouble again. And I've got a witness! Why don't I do it?" Gail seemed actually to be asking himself this question in deadly earnest.

"I'll tell you why you don't do it," Stagg said quickly in a nervous voice. "I'm not sayin' you could, understand, but *if* you could. . . ."

"You *know* I could!" Gail interjected sternly, his eyes flashing fire. "If you want to be sure of it . . . *draw!*"

Stagg's face went white under its tan, then darkened as he pressed his lips into a fine white line.

"There's a man not so far off who can identify you," he hissed. "You can't afford any more shootin' if you intend to *live* here. An' you can't afford to be identified as a member of that Trantler's outfit. The sheriff up here might try to protect you, but that sheriff down in Wyoming would think different. He's been seein' red ever since that hold-up. I don't reckon even the Keenes would front for an outlaw friend!"

Gail moved his horse closer to Stagg's mount. "Don't stir your right hand, Stagg!" he commanded. Fire flickered in his eyes. Suddenly he drew—swift as a wink of time, sure as light. His gun covered the startled ex-foreman. His voice trembled with the violence of his emotion.

"If I was sure what you say is true, Stagg, I'd shoot you down like the dog you are, so help me . . . so *help* me!" He struggled with what seemed to be an inclination to yield to impulse. "You had an idea about this in your head when you said I'd crawl to you to give you your job back. You don't want just what you think is a bribe. You want to run the Hanging X. You can't have the first, an' you can't do the second." Gail's eyes were blazing, his whole body was trembling, but his nerves were tense and the hand that held the gun was steady as steel.

"Who is this man you say can identify me as . . . what you said?" he demanded. "Tell me, Stagg, or *take* it!"

Stagg could almost see the bullet leaving the gun. He did not flinch, although he was powerless to move, so sure was he that Gail would shoot. "Name's Jordan," he said. "He was a look-out for the Big Horn."

Gail couldn't trust himself to cover Stagg longer. The world had gone blood red. Fury raged in his mind and in his heart. He could not bribe this man—could not bring himself to make any concession—but he *could* kill him!

"Get out of my sight!" he shouted hoarsely. "Get out or so help me, I'll. . . ."

Stagg whirled his horse and drove in his spurs, deathly white, as Gail fired. The bullet shrieked in his ears as he galloped madly away.

Gail rode down the road toward the distant Spencer and the ranch, still holding the warm gun in his hand, his brain whirling and his senses reeling in turmoil. Spencer had heard the shot and was riding back. He turned and galloped madly along with Gail. When he had recovered, and slowed the pace, Gail told him what had been said and described Stagg's narrow escape without further explanation.

Spencer said nothing, but his eyes were hard with the resolve to silence Stagg's tongue. His hand caressed his gun. Gail saw the look and the instinctive move of the hand.

"Get that out of your head, Spence," he said sharply. "If that had been in the picture, I wouldn't have missed!"

Sheriff Will Woods was in his office in the county jail at Riverhead at the close of the hot day. The office in the stone building was cool after sunset, and the sheriff liked to sit at his desk and smoke a cigar after supper in the gathering dusk. A scented breeze filtered through the branches of the trees and blew gently in the open window to stir papers on the desk.

The sheriff had much to think about these days, and considerable of his thinking was connected with Gail Landon and the Hanging X. The sheriff knew Gail had left the ranch three days before. He had had to guess at the reason for Gail's absence. He had written to the sheriff down in Graybolt informing him that the mystery of Cramer's death had been solved, apparently, but in no way linking it with the activities of Trantler's gang. Yes, the sheriff had plenty to think about—and to puzzle him.

A horseman rode up to the jail entrance, dismounted, tied his horse to the hitching rail, dusted off his sleeves and hat, and entered.

" 'Lo, Stagg," the sheriff greeted as the ex-foreman loomed in the open doorway of the office. "Hot day for ridin'. Come in."

Stagg closed the door after him and sat down across from the sheriff. He was frowning, but cool.

"Landon's back," he said succinctly, glancing sharply to see what effect this would have on Woods.

"Yes? Where's he back from?" the sheriff asked mildly.

"When I saw him, he was ridin' down from the north,

but that don't mean anything."

"It might," the sheriff observed. "He might have been up to the shipping point."

"He wouldn't be gone to the shippin' point for three days," Stagg scoffed. "He brought back a man with him."

Woods nodded with mild interest. "He said he was going to hire a man to help him run the ranch."

"He's hired a gunman, if I ever saw one sittin' in the saddle!"

"A gunman?" Sheriff Woods arched his brows in surprise. "Why, Gail doesn't need to hire a gunfighter. He's fast enough by himself."

"Might want one, just the same . . . to do the dirty work," Stagg hinted broadly.

The sheriff pushed back his hat and leaned his elbows on the desk. "I reckon that calls for more, Stagg."

"Don't you think I know why he fired me off the ranch?" Stagg flared. "He wants his own crowd in there an' I was too smart for him. I'd get wise to him too quick. When I say his own crowd, I mean the kind of people he's been trailin' with these past years. High riders an' outlaws, if you ask me, an' this new man I saw him with today is one of 'em!"

"You're talking a bit wild, Stagg," Woods reproved. "Do you know this man who was with him today? An' where'd you see them?"

"Out at Eleven Mile. I was headed for the ranch. I've been out there lookin' for Landon every day for three days. He was just gettin' back. No, I don't know the man who was with him, but one look was enough to stamp him as a high trailer to me." His eyes glowed fiery in the fading light.

"Be a little careful, Stagg," the sheriff warned. "Remember you're talking to me an' I'm. . . ."

"You're his friend!" Stagg interrupted. "You want to

protect him! Well, that's just why I came to you. I've been on a little trip myself, down south a ways . . . quite a long ways. I know a thing or two, Woods. It'd surprise you to know what I know. An' I know where there's a man middling close to here who can prove what I know. I got the thousand cash that old Nate left me, all right. Now I'll take a hundred dollars a head for the hundred head of stock that's coming to me. It mightn't be above what the cattle'll be worth as beef steers. Maybe you'll put a bug in his ear to cough up. That's straight. If he don't wise up to himself, or if somebody don't put a bug in his ear within three days, I'll put a bee where it'll sting him!" He rose, and kicked back his chair.

"Wait a minute, Stagg," said Woods. The sheriff remembered what the ex-foreman had told him the new hand had said about Gail's having been in the south and maybe running with Trantler. "What do you think you've got on Gail? You can tell me in confidence, can't you?"

"I can, but I won't," Stagg said harshly. "Ask him. He knows."

"Why didn't you tell him yourself?" Woods asked, scowling.

"I did, an' he wanted to try to swap shots with me. I'm too smart for that!"

"You better see Griffin," the sheriff advised.

"I said three days," Stagg gritted. "That means by the Fifth of July. That's all I've got to say."

The sheriff let him go. He took a fresh cigar from a box in the drawer of his desk. He smoked it thoughtfully until the office was dark and he could see the lights from the street through the trees. Then he got up and went out to see Griffin himself.

Chapter Nineteen

Gail's first thought, after he and Spencer had arrived at the ranch shortly after noon, was to question Luke Denan about Stagg's visits to the Hanging X.

"Didn't say nothin' out of the way," Luke told him. "Acted agreeable enough for all his hard looks. Just asked where you was at an' when you was comin' back. He was here yesterday an' the day before."

Spencer was putting up the horses while Gail talked with Luke.

"That Beasley showed up after you left that night," Luke volunteered before Gail could ask. "I sent him up to report to Chuck Clark, like you said to do."

"Didn't you ride up there with him?" Gail asked. "I wanted him watched."

"I trailed him an' kept him in sight, figuring if he made another break I'd foller him. He rode straight up to Clark. I asked him before he went why he had lit out in the first place, an' he said he didn't want no sheriffs lookin' him over. Said I should understand an' not say anything. I got an idea he's queer in the head."

"I've got a different idea," Gail said. "Ride up and tell Chuck I want to see him down here. Tell him to bring Beasley along."

Gail took Spencer in the house for dinner.

While they were eating, Gail told Spencer about Beasley,

who had told Stagg he had been in the south, and how he had fled rather than let the sheriff see him.

"Stagg hired him, you say?" Spencer asked pointedly.

"Yes," Gail answered, looking at him steadily. "I wonder if you're thinking along the same line as myself."

"If you're thinkin' that this Stagg got his first hint about Trantler from Beasley, we're both on the same track," Spencer said.

"Exactly!" Gail exclaimed. "I'm going to rake Beasley over the coals. What's more, I wouldn't be surprised if it was Beasley who's been spying on me, and doing it for Stagg."

"Now you're getting closer." Spencer nodded. "Let's go a little further than that. I can tell soon's I see him if this Beasley has ever run with Trantler's gang. If he quit 'em, he had a reason. If he's still on good terms with Trantler, an' in with Stagg, too . . . why . . . you see?"

Gail was staring with startled eyes. "You mean they might be linked up? No! Not with Stagg mentioning this Jordan. I don't think we can go that far." But Spencer's conjecture worried him just the same. "I'm going to keep Beasley the same as a prisoner here at the ranch an' see what happens," he announced.

"Or fire him an' follow him," Spencer suggested.

"I'll think that over, too," Gail said with a frown.

An hour after the late dinner Gail had a visitor. Spencer had gone with one of the hands to pick himself a saddle pony in the lower pasture. Gail came out of the house to the porch, and then ran down the steps into the courtyard to welcome Matt Keene, owner of the Bar 4.

Keene surveyed Gail from under his bushy brows with interest. He expressed his regret that the tragedy that had taken the lives of Gail's mother and stepfather had occurred and said he had been to the ranch before but had not found Gail at home. Gail said he was sorry this had been the case and invited the older stockman into the house. Keene preferred to sit on the porch.

"Doris expected you over to dinner yesterday, but I told her you had more on your mind than dinner invitations," he said casually.

"That's right! I'd forgotten . . . that is . . . I wasn't here," Gail stammered. The day before had been Sunday and he and Spencer had been on the train. "Tell her I was going to ask for a dance in town on the Fourth but I don't know if I'll be there. . . ." He stopped with a frown. Keene's look hadn't encouraged him to say more.

"I'll tell her you're busy," said the stockman. "Woods told me about the trouble you had out here the other day. None of us wants to see you get off on the wrong side of the hoss, Landon. I rode over today to tell you something an' to ask you something. First I want to ask if your stock is all right." He was looking at Gail searchingly. "Is it all there, I mean?"

"We took a count after I let Stagg go," Gail replied. "There wasn't a head missing." He was puzzled by Keene's grave manner.

"Is it all right to ask why you let Stagg go, Landon? I don't want to meddle. But you're an owner on this range now, an' that makes you a member of our Cattlemen's Association, an' anything you tell me will be held in strict confidence."

"I let him go because he as much as told me he'd run this ranch as he saw fit. I want it run as near like Nate Martin would run it as possible. Nate's methods were successful and Stagg wanted to change them. He didn't show a spirit of co-operation."

"Very well. That's a good answer." Keene gave evidence of being pleased. "Us old fellows had to figure things out the best way when runnin' stock wasn't as easy as it is now. But Landon, I've lost some cattle. A hundred an' ten head of beef steers vanished on my east range. Just evaporated, it looks like. Smoothest work I've heard of in years . . . unless it was planned on the inside, which I doubt. Run off since we made the spring count an' put the herd over there. That's why I asked you if you'd lost any cattle."

He looked hard at Gail, but the latter's eyes were wide with astonishment.

"You sure?" Gail gulped. Possibly because of what he and Spencer had been talking about, his thoughts were flashing in confusion to Stagg and Beasley.

"I would hardly come here an' tell you this if I didn't know what I was talkin' about," said Keene dryly. "You haven't lost any?"

"Not that I know of. Not unless they've been taken in the last three days or until I got back today. I've sent for Chuck Clark to come to the house. He'll know. Why, it doesn't hardly seem possible!"

"That's the way it looked to me," said Keene, rising from his chair. "But when you count stock yourself an' find there're a hundred an' ten head missing that should be there, why . . . what the hell! I must be riding back, Landon, but I'll come over again in a day or two. Meanwhile, you look around."

When Keene had gone, Gail stood bareheaded in the courtyard. As the warm sun poured down upon him, it seemed to burn a name into his brain. Trantler! Could it be that Trantler was really in the neighborhood, as Gail half suspected, and stealing cattle? A preliminary to a raid on Gail's stock? Possibly. But if the outlaw proposed to bother

Gail, why should he disturb Keene and set the Bar 4 outfit to looking around first? It would make his work more difficult. Gail couldn't forget that Trantler, according to all reports, had first started his outlaw career as a rustler and had been a clever cow thief. But Stagg had boasted that years ago he had been the same thing!

Gail went inside, got his hat, and was starting for his horse when Chuck Clark galloped into the courtyard with Luke.

"Met Luke ridin' up to get me," Clark said breathlessly as he dismounted and turned his reins over to Luke. "Beasley's beat it again. Did you see him ridin' west?"

"No," Gail replied angrily. "An' I came down from the north an' didn't see him up that way. An' Matt Keene's been here an' he didn't mention seeing anyone over toward his range, which, if he had, he would have investigated. I thought I told you to watch Beasley."

"I had him watched," Clark declared. "I put him with Joe on purpose. Joe watched him when he drifted away from the herd. He met Jim Stagg both times. Today I had Joe in with me a few minutes along about noon an' that's when Beasley beat it like a streak. He must have come down this way." Clark was mad rather than just simply exasperated.

"Then we're going to chase him up this time," Gail said grimly. "And what do you think? Keene says he's a hundred an' ten head of beeves short an' he thinks they've been run off."

Clark stared upon hearing this. "Business is picking up," was his comment.

"I've got a new man here, Chuck. His name is Spencer. He's down picking out a horse for himself. He knows the cow business and he's jake, understand? I had a run-in with

Stagg today when Spencer and I met him up at Eleven Mile. He was on his way here again. Says he wants a hundred dollars a head for the hundred head of two-year-olds he has coming. Don't laugh. He was rough about it. I got rough myself. He can't hold me up. This Beasley's been meeting him, you say? Then there's a connection between those two, just as I thought. I want Beasley!"

"I started down this way as soon as I learned he was gone," Clark said. "I sent Joe and another hand west and one man up to the spring. He didn't go east, but I shoved two men off that way. I met Luke an' headed for here. Beasley has beat it for the badlands."

"And maybe Keene's cattle are in the badlands!" Gail exclaimed. "Beasley popped out of sight as soon as I got back. Maybe he saw me coming. This is suspicious enough to make him our mark." He looked into the western sky where the sun hung in dazzling splendor, poised for its drop behind the mountains. "Clark, you go up and get a bunch of the men . . . all you can spare," he ordered. "See that you pick good riders and good shots. See that they're on fresh horses. You can't get back with them before dark, and we can't search the badlands at night, but have them here at daybreak. We're going to find this Beasley and anybody else who's hanging around."

As Clark left, Gail told Luke to saddle his best horse for him. Spencer arrived riding a horse he had roped in the pasture.

"You've sure got some nice stock, Landon," Spencer said with a friendly grin. He patted the horse on its neck. "I don't mean just cows, either."

"And you know good horseflesh when you see it," Gail said. "That was my second best." He grew serious as Spencer dismounted. "That man Beasley is missing," he said. Then he explained what he had learned from Clark. "Luke will be out with my horse in a minute and you an' I will take a look around."

"Say!" Spencer looked at him, deeply thoughtful, wrinkling his brows. "Didn't you say something about this Stagg wanting to run cattle in the bottoms or somewhere down here? Are any cattle supposed to be below the house?"

"No." Gail looked at him with a puzzled expression. "The herds are all north and off a bit east of here."

"It must have been an east herd I glimpsed from the lower pasture," said Spencer, looking about at the sky. "I'm none too sure of directions here yet an' I get turned around."

"You couldn't see any cattle from the pasture," Gail contradicted.

"No? Well, my eyes ain't that bad. I sure *did* see some, an' they looked good-sized an' fat to me. Off that way from below here." He flung an arm in a gesture toward the southeast.

Gail flashed a look to westward where the sun was dipping behind the mountains as if to make sure. "That way?" he said. "Why, the way you pointed would be down in the Corner. I had Clark take the cattle Stagg had in the Corner out of there."

Luke came up, leading his horse.

"Didn't Clark take the cattle out of the Corner, Luke . . . do you know?" Gail asked as he mounted.

"Sure he did," Luke confirmed.

Gail looked at Spencer, but Spencer was shaking his head.

"Come on an' we'll see," said Gail, shaking out his reins. "It's on our way."

They galloped down past the pasture and above the

191

hayfield. Gail pulled his horse up with an exclamation of astonishment.

"There is a herd there!" he shouted in astonishment. "An' they're beef steers or I'm. . . ." He cut his words off short and they raced their horses toward the herd.

But before they reached the herd their practiced eyes had estimated the number of steers.

"How many would you say were there?" Gail asked.

"A hundred or so," Spencer answered without hesitation.

Gail sat his horse, looking intently at the grazing cattle, and told Spencer of Matt Keene's visit and his report about missing stock. "We'll look at the brand!" he concluded, and they rode on.

Gail needed but two or three glances to make sure of what he saw. "What do you make of it, Spence?" he asked, dumbfounded.

"A hundred an' ten head of Bar Four steers," Spencer said. "I reckon this is the bunch Keene missed."

"But why . . . how . . . ?" Gail's words trailed off. He was looking at the gap in the timber that marked the road to the river ford in the badlands.

"The rustlers shoved 'em on to your range, thinking they'd. . . ." Spencer stopped as a shout came from Gail.

Gail was suddenly riding toward the gap in the trees, urging his horse with spur, hand, and voice. Spencer tore after him, but Gail had the start of him and kept ahead. Spencer now saw what Gail had glimpsed a few moments before. A rider was pushing his horse along the edge of the trees in an easterly direction.

When Gail first had caught sight of the horseman, the latter had been on the road to the ford. As Gail rode toward him, the rider had darted from the road to the open plain at the edge of the timber that screened the badlands. The rider was speeding frantically, pausing momentarily now and then, it seemed, as though he were looking for a trail into the river brakes.

A rosy glow had come over the land with the sunset, but in the ravines in the badlands and the labyrinths of dim trails it would be gloomy; soon it would be almost dark in those fastnesses. Gail urged his splendid horse to its utmost, and finally, as he gained rapidly on the fugitive, he recognized the fleeing rider as Beasley.

He shouted as he bore down upon him. Then Beasley found an opening and turned his horse into the trees. Gail soon reached the spot and waved to Spencer who was following like the wind. As Gail's mount plunged into the narrow trail that Beasley had taken, a spurt of flame licked from the shadows ahead.

Gail's gun snapped into his hand and he turned his horse in a stout pull as Beasley fired again. There were branches, leaves between Gail and his quarry, but Gail saw the bullet clip a twig, and then a fitful gleam from the crimson skies shot into the shadows and lighted the twisted features of Beasley, his eyes burning and narrowly squinted.

Gail fired just as a third bullet cut through the foliage.

Beasley's horse leaped and its rider plunged to the dirt trail as Spencer brought his horse to a halt behind Gail.

"Look out for the others!" Gail shouted as he dismounted to examine Beasley.

Spencer turned his horse partly so he had a view of the trail in both directions. His gun was out. When he next glanced down at Gail, he saw him binding a handkerchief about Beasley's head. Gail looked up presently.

"Grazed him," he said crisply. "I'll carry him on my horse with me to the house. We've got to get there before dark."

Shortly afterward they rode out upon the plain, Gail carrying the limp form of Beasley in front of him in the saddle, and Spencer, his gun ready, his eyes gleaming with their old cold glint, bringing up the rear.

Chapter Twenty

Beasley opened his eyes covertly several times on the ride back to the ranch, but they were closed when Gail carried him into the bunkhouse and put him down. Spencer turned the horses over to Luke and brought water and bandages from the house as well as a first-aid kit.

"Pshaw," said Gail as he worked over Beasley. "That bullet just scraped the hair off. It wasn't enough to put him out like this. Here . . . look here, Spence! See this bump on the back of his head? He got that when his horse threw him. He's just stunned. Call to Luke to bring in a couple of pails of cold water." He shook Beasley.

Before Spencer could call to Luke, the wounded man opened his eyes. He raised a hand weakly and whispered for water.

"Here," said Gail, holding a cup of water to the man's lips. "You're all right. You're not even nicked. You bumped your head on a rock when you fell off your horse. Drink that water and tell us what you were doing with those Bar Four cattle."

Beasley's eyes were wide and clear enough now.

"I wasn't with those cattle," he said in a high-pitched voice.

"Then what were you doing down there?" Gail demanded.

"I was startin' back for the ranch when I saw somebody

with the cattle an' I thought I better not be seen around there," Beasley replied.

Gail looked at Spencer with a grim smile. "Sit down, Spence. I'm going to give this fellow just five minutes to talk and tell plenty." He looked narrowly at the startled Beasley who was pale and nervous.

"You saw *me,* didn't you, Beasley? You must have wanted to get away from me pretty bad to resort to your gun! I suppose you think I feel sorry for you because you took three shots at me! Why did you do it?"

"I couldn't see good in there. My eyes ain't too good. I wasn't sure it was you, an' I didn't know what I was doing."

"Four lies in a row!" Gail exclaimed. "I'll be fair, Beasley. I'll give you a chance to lie four more times before I turn you over to the sheriff! Maybe you'll be able to explain to the sheriff and Matt Keene and his foreman, Red Snyder, how you came to be working around those stolen steers down there and what you were doing with the running irons and other tools we're going to find down there."

"I didn't have no runnin' irons!" shouted Beasley, rising up on the bunk.

"I said the running irons we are *going* to find." Gail smiled. "If I have to, I'll link you up with those stolen steers tighter than you are. But you're in a bad spot as it is. Matt Keene was over here today complaining." He rolled a cigarette.

Beasley's eyes were snapping. "You ain't got as much on me as you think!" he growled.

"No?" Gail lighted his smoke. "I've got more on you than *you* think. You spotted me up at Eleven Mile Spring the first day I came. You took the word to Stagg. You followed me when I left here four nights ago. You sneaked off yesterday and the day before to meet Stagg. I reckon you thought you were doing all the spying on this ranch. You probably believed Stagg when he told you I couldn't look out for myself, or something like that."

Beasley showed by his look that this bothered him. He remained silent.

"Aside from your finding it pretty hard to explain what you were doing around that stolen herd, I reckon Stagg will find it hard to prove *he* didn't have anything to do with it. I'm thinking you've been working for Stagg instead of me. Isn't that so?"

"I haven't got any money from anybody yet!" Beasley snarled.

"Well, you're not going to get any from Stagg!" Gail waited for this to sink in. "I'll pay your wages up to now if you'll do one thing." Gail's look and tone hardened. "You can do only one of two things, Beasley, and I'm not playing you for a fool, or I wouldn't bother talking to you. You can come clean. That's one way out. Or you can go to jail charged with stealing cattle and with criminal assault with a gun with intent to kill. That means trouble."

"Stagg would have something to say about that!" Beasley's eyes seemed to be playing hide-and-seek with his dark thoughts.

Gail shook his head. "You're not fool enough to depend on Stagg. He'll have enough explaining to do on his own hook without bothering about you. You were just his tool, Beasley. He'd have thrown you over, anyway."

"He's got plenty on you!" Beasley blurted unwittingly.

Gail shot a quick look at Spencer, and then laughed.

"Has he been telling you that story, Beasley?" he said scornfully. Gail had sensed immediately that Stagg had told the man enough to make him think he could get money by helping him in some way. "Did he take you in on that? Did he tell you that rigmarole about me being mixed up in something awful down south and that I'd pay?" He laughed again, partly at the look of blank astonishment that appeared on Beasley's face. "I chased Stagg off with a gun today," he added coldly. "If you'd ridden west when you sneaked away up there today, you'd have seen me do it! Does that sound like I was afraid of Stagg?"

"I didn't have anything to do with those cattle," Beasley grumbled. "I've got a right to ride off the ranch . . . to quit . . . if I want to."

"But you haven't got any right to shoot at me," said Gail, turning to Spencer. "Call Luke, Spence."

"What're you callin' him for?" Beasley asked quickly as Spencer stepped to the door.

Gail walked around the table in the center of the room, smoking, making no answer.

"Look here, you can't bluff me," said Beasley, sitting up.

"No one is trying to bluff you, Beasley," Gail told him coolly. "You had your chance. I've decided you're a fool, after all."

Luke Denan entered as Spencer stepped away from the door.

"Luke, sit down and see that this man doesn't get off that bunk while Spencer and I go to supper," said Gail. "There's nothing wrong with him except a bump on the head and a lack of brains inside it. Let him talk, but don't answer him. When we come back, you can hitch the team to the buckboard. I'm taking him to the sheriff tonight."

Beasley was calling to them when Gail and Spencer went out the door.

When the two returned to the bunkhouse after supper, Gail brought some coffee and food for Beasley. "Don't tell 'em I didn't feed you out here," he said, placing Beasley's supper on a chair by the bed. "Stagg will maybe be in jail with you. . . . Luke, hitch up the team."

Beasley drank some of the coffee after Luke went out.

"I reckon you and Luke will have to keep an eye on Keene's cattle," Gail said to Spencer. "The sheriff may come out with me in the morning."

"Look here!" Beasley exploded. "I ain't going to take the blame for this!"

Gail watched Spencer light the lamp on the table. Neither spoke.

"Stagg's behind this business!" Beasley declared harshly.

"He'll be glad to hear you say that," Gail said dryly.

"He took those steers, I tell you!" cried Beasley. "Snyder let him do it! They've been thick all spring, them two. Stagg was goin' to make it look like you took 'em if you didn't kick in!"

"There's a story!" Gail scoffed. "How'd they get where they are? Stagg rode off to town after I chased him away this afternoon. He couldn't get around there to drive 'em into the Corner this quick."

"You think I did it?" Beasley shouted. It made him furious to think he wasn't believed when he had made up his mind to get out of the mess the best he could.

"Of course, you did it," said Gail in a tone of contempt.

"I tell you I didn't do it! The cattle were there when I rode down. I went into the badlands to see if Stagg was there. When I didn't see him, I came back. At first I thought you was Stagg. If I'd known it was you, I wouldn't have got caught. Stagg *must* have put 'em there!" Despite the hoarseness of his voice the ring of truth was there.

"Who else besides you or Stagg could have done it?" Gail demanded coldly.

"Snyder, maybe. He wanted to help Stagg. They're thick. Stagg had that herd of two-year-olds down there because he was goin' to sneak 'em off a hundred at a time, an', if he got caught, he could say he was takin' the stock that'd been left to him."

Both Gail and Spencer saw at once that there was something to this.

"Were you coming back to the ranch . . . later?" Gail asked.

"No. I had to go. . . ." Beasley checked himself and a look of cunning brimmed in his eyes.

The sounds of horses being hooked up to the buckboard came from outside. Gail rose. "I can't trust you," he said. He stepped to the door. "Call me when you're ready, Luke!" he shouted.

"No!" cried Beasley, swinging his feet over the side of the bunk. His face was contorted with a mixture of fear and rage. "I guess you know enough so you got me cornered . . . an' Stagg, too!" he said hoarsely. Then he let out a string of oaths. "You said if I came clean, I'd get out of it," he accused in a pleading voice.

"But you haven't come clean," Gail said.

There was a sound of wheels in the courtyard. "All ready!" came Luke's voice.

"What I've said is the truth!" yelled Beasley. "Listen!" He wiped the beads of sweat from his forehead and lowered his tone. "I was goin' to the cabin . . . the old nester cabin, they call it . . . five miles west of here on the river. The old ford, you know? Where that south road comes down from town. Maybe it's farther than that. It's the only cabin on the river. . . ."

"I know where it is," Gail broke in impatiently.

"I was goin' there. Stagg's got a man holed up there."

"I know," said Gail, leaping to conclusions, "short, slim fellow. Snaky sort. Two-gun man." He was sure it was Jordan.

"That's him," Beasley nodded eagerly. "Comes from Wyoming. I've been packing grub down to him. I heard Stagg call him Jordan. That's where I was goin' to meet Stagg. Now that's all I know, s'help me! Stagg was goin' to give me three hundred dollars to tell him what was goin' on here an' to help him with the cattle if he had to use 'em. He said he'd give me a job afterward. He said he wasn't goin' to be bossed by no . . . by you. Do you believe me?" His last words rose to a shriek of frenzy.

Gail believed him, but he didn't intend to tell him so.

"I'm not going to take you in to the sheriff, Beasley," he said slowly, "but I'm going to keep you here till I've checked up on what you've told me. If you've told me the truth, I'll do what I can for you. That's a promise. Eat your supper and get some sleep. Luke will look after you, and, if you try any tricks, he'll pop you."

"What do you think?" Gail asked Spencer a little later when they were in the courtyard.

"I think he was scared enough to tell the truth," Spencer said bluntly. "I never saw him before, but I know his kind. He tried to pot you, didn't he? He's got some kind of a nasty record. I'm goin' to ride over to that cabin an' see if Jordan's there. I can find the place all right an' I've got the timber along the river to guide me. We might as well know for sure about that end of it. Beasley didn't move those cattle alone. Stagg couldn't have got around there so quick. Maybe Jordan was helpin' 'em. I'll find out." He started for the barn.

"I'll go with you," Gail decided.

Spencer argued hotly as they saddled their horses, and in the end he won. Gail left his saddled horse in its stall.

"You've got to see that Beasley doesn't sneak away by some trick," Spencer pointed out. "An' the way news travels around here, Stagg might hear somehow an' show up here."

It wasn't until after Spencer had ridden away under the first stars that Gail was struck dumb by the surmise that Spencer might intend deliberately to put Jordan out of the way if he found him!

Norm Spencer, riding next to the dark shadow of the trees on the bank of the river, caught a faint glimmer of light through interlaced branches as he reached the little-used road to the old ford. He tied his horse in the trees and stole softly to where the yellow rays of lamplight glowed dully behind greased paper substituting for glass in the window of the cabin. He glued his eyes to a single crack in the paper and waited until the occupant of the cabin came within his narrow range of vision for a moment. Then he straightened and drew back. Behind the cabin a horse stood in a makeshift corral. Jordan—for it was the former lookout—was alone.

Spencer forgot that he had come merely to ascertain if the man Beasley had told the truth. Jordan constituted the real menace. He slipped around to the door. He tried the latch. It gave. The door opened, and Spencer stepped just inside as Jordan whirled. Then Spencer saw that Jordan's upper right side seemed bulky as if it were bandaged.

"Hello," Spencer said. "Campin' out on your way through?" He looked at the scant store of supplies on the table and shelf. A lantern on the table supplied the light. The stove was hot and there was an aroma of coffee in the room.

Jordan was frowning, gazing keenly at Spencer with a puzzled light in his eyes.

"I've seen you some place," he said. He had, as Spencer knew, seen him in the Big Horn resort in Graybolt before the raid. But he could not have known Spencer later when he was masked and moving swiftly. Jordan had seen hundreds of men. He could not always place a face properly in his mind.

"No stranger around here, then?" Spencer said, closing the door behind him.

"What do you want?" Jordan demanded.

"I want to know what you're doin' here," Spencer said sternly.

A flicker of apprehension showed in Jordan's eyes as he saw the other's change of manner. He strove to place this man in his mind. Then it came to him that his visitor might be one of the outlaws.

"I'm passing through, like you said," he got out slowly. His left hand was caressing the right lapel of his coat.

"You'll have to do better than that," Spencer said sharply. He was watching that left hand. "Rustlers have been operatin' just west of here an' maybe that lets you in."

Jordan's face cleared. "That lets me out, you mean," he said. "I'm not mixed up with any rustling an' I can prove it."

"How?" Spencer put the word like the crack of a whiplash. A great idea had come to him. He could compel Jordan to go with him to the ranch and thus ascertain if Jordan could recognize Gail Landon.

"Why . . . ," Jordan hesitated, his eyes narrowing. He could not be sure to whom he was talking. "Are you a stockman, a 'puncher, or a deputy . . . or what?" he demanded.

"I'm workin' on a ranch," Spencer told him. "What's your name, where are you from, an' what're you doin' here? You're not just passing through by the looks of things here." He indicated the supplies. "You've been here a few days."

"I'll go right on in to town with you, if you want," said Jordan coolly.

Jordan had played it safe. He had told the sheriff of Graybolt about Stagg. He had ridden north with Stagg, arriving three days ago, with the knowledge that the Graybolt sheriff was coming to Riverhead. Big rewards had been offered for Trantler and for the capture of any or all members of the outlaw band. It was one or more of these rewards that Jordan wanted—enough for a good stake. He was using Stagg as a means to an end. But if there was a member of Trantler's band in these parts, there might be more of them. This man before him might be one of them!

"What do you want to go to town for?" Spencer asked.

"To the sheriff, if you say so, or if you think I'm a rustler," Jordan sneered.

"We don't have to go to town for that," Spencer said curtly. "Get your hat. We'll ride over to the ranch, an' . . . no, you don't!"

Spencer leaped like a tiger as Jordan's left hand plunged inside his coat. Spencer caught Jordan's wrist, snapped it down with a twist, and a gun rattled on the floor. Spencer locked his left arm about Jordan's neck to hold him. He drew a second gun from Jordan's waistband, then flung him back against the wall.

"So that's the way it is," he said grimly. He picked up the other weapon and threw both guns into a corner. "What did you want to get the drop on me for, if you're straight? No answer? Well, we'll go!"

But at that moment the pound of hoofs and the snort of a horse sounded outside. Spencer stepped toward the door, turned in time to clamp a hand over Jordan's mouth, stifling a shout, backed away as the door was flung open.

It was Stagg.

The ex-foreman stepped into the light with a wicked look in his eyes. He appeared to sense the situation at once, although Jordan's expression was one of relief rather than of warning.

"The new hand," Stagg purred so that his voice seemed to hiss in the room. It was as if he had thrown off a mask he had worn for years. "Just ridin' around?" he sneered.

"He thinks I'm a rustler," Jordan put in. For a fleeting moment he felt a prick of suspicion. Could this be a frame-up? His alarm was dissipated with the next words that came from Spencer.

"I think you're one, too!" Spencer said bluntly. Here was a situation he could handle. He saw the rage flaming in Stagg's eyes as Stagg fancied his schemes were being frustrated. Then he tensed as he saw a resolve gleam coldly and deadly in Stagg's gaze.

"You think that's an alibi?" Stagg cried harshly. "I think Landon hired you as a sneak, instead of a gunman. One of the crowd he ran with down south! One of Trantler's bunch, maybe!"

This was a random shot, but Stagg's eyes sparked a warning. In the moment he said it, he believed it.

"Put 'em up!" he roared, his hand darting swiftly.

But Spencer had seen the draw coming, had sensed it with unerring instinct. His weapon blazed at his waist as Stagg's hand came up.

The ex-foreman's gun spun to the floor and Stagg turned as a bullet smashed through his arm. A cry of pain was followed by a volley of oaths.

"You can blame this on Beasley!" rang Spencer's voice.

In a wink of silence Spencer again caught the sound of hoof beats. This time he took no chance. He darted through the door and into the deep shadow as three horsemen approached the cabin. In the starlight Spencer glimpsed the gleam of a silver badge.

"Watch out, Sheriff!" Jordan shouted in the cabin doorway.

Spencer quickly slipped through the trees to his horse.

Chapter Twenty-One

Gail Landon rode down to the Corner with two of the hands who were working in the field in the bottoms. He left them there to watch the stolen Bar 4 herd and rode back past the hay sheds and south camp to the house. He didn't unsaddle his horse, for he intended to go abroad again this night. He decided to leave a note on the table in the living room stating where he was bound as a precaution against his possible disappearance: for he intended to search a portion of the badlands alone.

The bunkhouse windows were lighted faintly by a lamp turned low. The others in the ranch house were asleep when Gail entered. He wrote the brief note in the office, scribbled: **Clark or Spencer** on the envelope, and took it out into the living room. As he put it on the table under the shaded lamp, the flutter of a curtain at an open window attracted his attention. The breeze was freshening from the west.

He decided to open the window. He took one step and froze, motionless, every nerve tense. He had heard a sound at the door, the *rasp* of the knob as it turned, a *creak* as the door opened. A current of air blew the ends of the curtain outside the window.

"Take it easy!" came the sibilant warning, but the voice thundered familiarly in Gail's ears.

He turned quickly to face Trantler—waspish, lean-faced,

leering, and triumphant—quietly closing the door.

That first instantaneous reading of the evil look in the outlaw's eyes convinced Gail that, as he had told Beasley some time before, there was but one way out. In Gail's case this meant the wiping out of Trantler. The realization left him pale, but calm.

"I've been expecting you," he said coolly.

Trantler stepped as far as the table, the green lights between his narrowed lids flickering balefully. "Did Slossom tell you?" he asked, his lower lip curling against yellow teeth.

"No. But I wouldn't have to be told, since Slossom knew. . . ."

Trantler held up his slim, smooth gun hand. "Slossom was a fool, Landon. I let him go ahead. You finished him an' saved me the trouble. He wasn't smart when he had to do his own thinking. He was using a club. I come to use your common sense. You have it nice, Landon"—he waved a hand about the comfortable room—"an' you want to keep it nice. Isn't that so?"

It wasn't what the bandit said so much as it was his tone and look which made Gail rigid. Here was a threat in chosen, silky words that hit like a sledge-hammer.

"What do you want?" Gail asked, struggling to control his voice.

"Something you can give with no loss to yourself," was the answer in a hoarse whisper. "I don't blame you for sneaking out after the . . . the morning after Graybolt. I got the truth from Slossom. But you must be careful. Not one of the men with me knows it's you who's here. I'm protecting you so you can play safe. You can work with me on a last job without takin' chances or . . . money profits. But then you won't see me again an' that's worth something." A horrible leer went with this.

Gail was puzzled, and he felt himself in a trap. He had no doubt but that Trantler's men were near. The boldness of the outlaw in coming to the house showed that he feared nothing.

"Go on," he invited coldly.

"This is the Second of July, you remember? We were to meet somewhere else but you didn't wait to learn more. No matter. This is better. There is money in Riverhead . . . much more money." Trantler tried to smile with hideous result.

"You know the ropes up here," he hissed. "You can steer me. No need to wait for the Fourth, an' too many in town then. Riverhead is bigger than Graybolt. You can come with us an' we'll move in there tomorrow night!"

"But how about your men seeing me?" Gail said in a panic. If Trantler kidnapped him, he would be powerless to help himself—and he would never come out alive! He didn't have to be told that; he could see it in those fiendish eyes. One chance. He must draw with Trantler. It was like looking into the ghastly face of Death itself.

"You will be with me," the outlaw said, frowning. "When the time comes that the others might see you, you can wear a full mask. I will take care of that."

"But I can't go tonight, Trantler. There's a reason. Some cattle have been stolen from the next ranch. They're looking for the rustlers. I'd be missed too quick and an alarm would go out. They'd comb the range, the river brakes, be on the look-out in town . . . swarm everywhere. I couldn't go before. . . ."

"Enough!" Trantler fairly spat the word. "I found the cattle in the brakes an' had 'em driven back on to the range so no one would be huntin' for 'em. They'll find 'em an' it'll give 'em something to think about. While they're thinking, we'll be working!"

Gail couldn't help staring as he heard this explanation of how the Bar 4 had suddenly appeared in the Corner. But Beasley had been down there, too. Could there be a connection . . . ?

Trantler's roving eyes had strayed to the table where the note Gail had written reposed in its envelope. He read the inscription.

"Clark or Spencer?" he said. "Is Spencer here?"

"There's a Spencer working on the ranch," Gail answered. "Now listen, Trantler. . . ." But he couldn't divert the outlaw's attention.

Trantler picked up the envelope, keeping his eyes on Gail. He opened it with his left hand and shook out the folded sheet of paper. He raised the paper to a level with his eyes, but to one side so he could catch sight of the slightest movement on Gail's part.

Now, then, Gail thought, *here's my chance to draw.*

But he had underestimated Trantler's quickness of eye. The outlaw had caught the four words—**gone into the brakes**—and this was enough.

The note fluttered to the floor.

"You were goin' into the brakes," Trantler sneered. "Why? To look for the rustlers? Bah! Spencer *is* here. You must have framed it with him to come here. Bought him off! Maybe you knew I was around. That's it! Maybe you've got a trap set somewheres. Where's Spencer?"

"He isn't here," Gail answered sharply. He wondered if sufficient time had passed for Spencer to complete his errand. It must be midnight. He had spent some time in the Corner; Spencer would be too cautious to ride into any trap.

"That's a lie!" Trantler accused, a murderous look in his snapping eyes. "All right! He can stay here, but you're goin' with me!"

Gail knew Trantler would draw and demand his gun. He would compel him to accompany him. Gail's whole nervous and muscular fiber tensed for the test. And here came an interruption that gave both of them pause. The courtyard swelled with sound; horses were there and men speaking; horses milling, pounding, snorting as they were pulled up.

In that moment Gail drew. Trantler's own hand whipped, but his left jerked out, also, striking the lamp from the table. It went down on the floor with a crash as the guns roared, spurting flame and rocking the room.

Gail drove for the floor, shooting at the door. He wriggled in the shadow to escape the bullets that Trantler fired at the red flashes. A chorus of shouts came from the courtyard and Gail heard Clark's voice. A shadow momentarily shut out the light in the open window. Gail fired, but the window was clear. Trantler had leaped through.

Gail jerked the door open as Clark came up the steps.

"Outlaws!" Gail cried hoarsely. "They must be below the house. They'll make for the brakes. After 'em!"

But Clark was bounding down the steps shouting his orders. He had not once forgotten what Gail had told him about the bandit in the south. He had expected something like this.

Gail ran through the house and out the rear. It was a matter almost of moments until he had secured his horse, which he had left saddled. He could hear Clark and the men spreading out, riding hard. Then came the first shots. The cowpunchers had sighted the outlaws!

Gail mounted and galloped around the barn, where a road cut down into the bottoms. When he reached the first field, he cut to the left, for the firing was coming from the east. It was in this direction that the hayfield was located, with the Corner beyond, offering good footing for running horses.

Presently Gail saw horsemen ahead and then a small, humped figure in the saddle swept from the shadows and cut across the field. Gail spurred his horse, recognizing the rider. It was Trantler. The outlaws were in full flight across the field in the moonlight. They were nine in number—the pick of Trantler's band.

The Hanging X riders came plunging through the scattered trees to the field as Gail rode up. "Spread out!" he cried to Clark. "See! They've taken to the hay sheds."

This was true. The outlaws had ridden into the big sheds and their guns were blazing from the shadows. As Gail looked, one of his men toppled from his saddle and fell. A horse, hit by a bullet, reared and went down. No make-believe shooting this, no scaring off! Gail slipped from his horse and started across the hayfield afoot. He was west of the sheds. The wind was blowing strongly from the west.

The Hanging X outfit had retreated but had formed a semicircle about the entrances to the shed which faced north. Beyond them on the east was the open range in the Corner. The outlaws could not leave the sheds without having to make a dash for it through a possible hail of lead. But Gail, stooping low and running through the field west of the sheds, knew Trantler had shot his way through many a posse more experienced than the range riders. He knew, too, that Trantler would drive his men ahead of him, would sacrifice every one of them if necessary to save his own skin. Cornered, Trantler seemed to possess the cunning madness and the luck of the devil. He had boasted of this luck. He had faith in it. It came near being his god!

Gail crept through the grass to the first shed. He could hear loud voices within, but none was the voice of Trantler. The firing was dying down. Damage had been done, but how much could not be estimated. Three riderless horses were circling about in front of the sheds.

Loose hay was lying about the side of the shed. There was some hay left in the sheds and the sheds themselves were dry as tinder. Gail hesitated. His thoughts raced back to the Big Horn raid. He had been in it and he had done his part. But he hadn't been allowed to let it go at that. First had come Slossom. Now came Trantler. If Trantler escaped, it meant the end of everything for Gail, for the outlaw would hound him to his death at the point of a flaming gun. Help him pull off a robbery in Riverhead? Go back to the danger trail?

Disgust seized Gail with such throbbing power it almost blinded him for a moment; disgust with himself for having been a fool to associate with the outlaw; disgust with Trantler as the symbol of a nefarious trade; disgust because he himself had indirectly brought this raid upon a peaceful range. He would drive Trantler out and settle with him, eye to eye, gun to gun—*any* way!

He bent low, struck a match, and applied it to the loose hay. The wind caught up the spark of fire, and, as Gail retreated a short distance, the flames spread about the hay, licked at the wood, blazed, and then roared up the side and over the shed, sending fiery brands to ignite the other shed.

The field, the entrances to the sheds, the riders in the circle, a part of the Corner, and even the distant stolen herd of cattle were lighted up by the lurid glare of the raging flames. A great shout went up from the riders as they saw Gail, but it died instantly lest it betray his position. He could not be seen from the front of the sheds. He was waiting for the break that had to come.

A chorus of yells came from the sheds. Smoke was pouring into them as the fire ate its way between the rough boards. Another yell came from the riders. Gail saw a horseman bearing straight across the field toward him. He tried to wave a warning. It was Spencer!

Then came the break. With red flames licking at the heavens and a saffron-colored pall of smoke hanging in the sky over the scene, the outlaws urged their horses out of the sheds and dashed toward the Corner.

Gail had run out into the glare in front of the sheds. As he had expected, Trantler spurred his horse with his own men between him and the Hanging X riders. But Clark and several others had spurred for the Corner to cut the outlaws off. They were shooting furiously. Spencer turned his horse straight ahead, his gun barking. Two of the outlaws' horses went down. A pile-up threatened.

But Trantler already had turned back and was racing for the end of the sheds with Gail directly in his path. He saw Gail and Spencer almost at the same moment. But he had seen Spencer first! His gun had whipped over. He flung himself on his horse's neck as he fired at Spencer, and the quick move, coming as his horse veered, flung him from the saddle. He seemed to twist in the air to land on his feet!

Gail caught a glimpse even in that tremendous moment of other riders galloping across the field, their faces clear in the light from the fire. Sheriff Woods, Griffin, a bearded man in an enormous hat, and the pale face of Jordan, the look-out!

"It's Trantler!" Jordan shrilled above the pounding of hoofs, the shouts, and the roar of the flames leaping like crimson demons into the hideous sky.

Then Gail saw Trantler, his gun in his hand at his thigh,

his eye blazing their message of swift, hot death.

"Drop it, Trantler!" he cried.

"Take it!" Trantler roared like thunder, his lungs seeming to burst with the ferocity of his terrible voice.

The fire struck a spark of red from Gail's gun as it leaped forward and cracked sharply with its speeding bullet. Trantler's shot stung Gail's ear with its whining whistle. The outlaw stumbled forward, shooting again as Gail leaped aside. Then he steadied, wavered like a reed in the wind, and crumpled in a heap as the sheriff and others closed in.

Gail looked up, white-faced and staring, at the red tongues making a frightful carnival in the sky. Then he flung his gun on the ground.

Chapter Twenty-Two

The bright morning sun shone through the vines and scattered golden spangles on the porch of the Hanging X ranch house. Gail Landon was sitting there alone. He had much on his mind, but it was singularly calm. His brain was marveling at the events of the night before, reviewing the happenings of the early morning as though he were situated apart from all that had taken place.

He had heard Jordan tell the bearded stranger, who had proved to be Sheriff Nixon of Graybolt, that he was entitled to a share of the rewards offered for Trantler and other members of the band who had been killed or captured. He had heard Nixon assure him he would get his share. He had been present when Beasley, reassured by Sheriff Woods, had told his story implicating Stagg and Red Snyder, the Bar 4 foreman, but clearing them and himself of any connection with Trantler. He had listened to Sheriff Woods explain that Stagg had been wounded by Spencer and that he was ready to take a fair price for the stock he had coming and leave the country, hoping Gail wouldn't prosecute. Gail had agreed.

Matt Keene had ridden over that morning and had been accompanied by Doris, who, he had said, had insisted on coming. He had heard Beasley explain about the cattle and had been satisfied, saying he would take the business up with Snyder and see that he showed more brains in the future. Doris was in the house with Mrs. Birch.

Spencer was in bed with a wound from Trantler's gun. The doctor was at the ranch attending those who required his services. Gail, by some queer twist of coincidence or arrangement, had not come face to face with Jordan. Clark and some of the men had gone to town with the prisoners, none of whom had seen Gail to identify him, so far as Gail knew.

Sheriff Woods and Griffin came up on the porch.

"That sheriff from Wyoming, Nixon," said Woods, clearing his throat, "wants this feller Jordan to take a look at you, Gail. Wants to see if Jordan knows you, I reckon. Here they come."

Gail frowned and looked quickly at Griffin, who didn't appear worried.

"Well, Jordan," said Nixon, stroking his beard and speaking in a deep voice, "do you know this young rancher?"

Jordan gazed at Gail, who eyed him curiously.

"He's the second man I've seen up here who looks like somebody I've seen before," said Jordan, "but I'm not sure." He wrinkled his brows. "No, I can't seem to put my finger on him."

"Well, then, we'll get ready to go into town," Nixon boomed.

They went away with Sheriff Woods, and Gail beckoned to Griffin as the lawyer started to go after them.

"That fellow knows me an' you know it," Gail accused.

"And he knows when he has enough," Griffin said. "He falls into quite a chunk of money, and I made it plain that you wanted no part of any rewards. After all, you risked your life with Trantler. Sheriff Nixon is satisfied with that and everything else. Sheriff Woods and I knew more than you thought and we knew it had to come. Stagg is satisfied to get off as well as he is doing. And what do you think you're paying me a retainer fee for? I'm your lawyer!"

"Humph," Gail said. "Your next job is to boost the price of beef."

Matt Keene came up the steps as Griffin left. He looked at Gail curiously and with just a glimmer of respect.

"How you doing?" he asked casually.

"Queer," Gail confessed. "Drunk with excitement, I guess." He leveled a steady look at the older stockman. "I reckon all this is pretty bad for me," he said.

"I wouldn't say that," said Keene, putting a hand on his shoulder. "When a man starts new in the business, he's got to have trouble an' learn. Old Nate found that out an' so did I. You walked into trouble down below an' it walked right back on you up here. You simply had to sit an' wait for it to come, I might say. But you'll pull through . . . with hard work."

Doris came out on the porch from inside the house.

Matt Keene scowled with mock severity. "You learned a lot of high-sounding words in school, Doris," he said. "Suppose you read Gail Landon a lecture on evil ways."

He went into the house for a cup of coffee.

"What does he mean by that?" Gail asked, looking up at her.

"When Daddy is hard put for something to say, he talks in riddles," Doris replied.

Gail rose quickly and pulled a chair close to his own.

"Let's sit down and talk about the dance in town tomorrow," he suggested, his spirits rising. "I haven't any troubles to tell. . . ."

"But I have!" Doris laughed. "Some other time," she added.

They sat down there on the porch, sheltered by the green vines, with golden sunshine flooding the world beyond the steps.

About the Author

Robert J. Horton was born in Coudersport, Pennsylvania. As a very young man he traveled extensively in the American West, working for newspapers. For several years he was sports editor for the *Great Falls Tribune* in Great Falls, Montana. He began writing Western fiction for *Adventure* magazine before becoming a regular contributor to Street & Smith's *Western Story Magazine*. By the mid-1920s Horton was one of three authors to whom Street & Smith paid 5¢ a word—the other two being Frederick Faust, perhaps better known as Max Brand®, and Robert Ormond Case. Many of Horton's serials for Street & Smith's *Western Story Magazine* were subsequently brought out as books by Chelsea House, Street & Smith's book publishing company. Although virtually all of Horton's stories appeared under his byline in the magazine, for their book editions Chelsea House published them either as by Robert J. Horton or by James Roberts. Sometimes, as was the case with *Rovin' Redden* (Chelsea House, 1925) by James Roberts, a book would consist of three short novels that were editorially joined to form a "novel". Other times the stories were serials published in book form, such as *Whispering Cañon* (Chelsea House, 1925) by James Roberts or *The Man of the Desert* (Chelsea House, 1925) by Robert J. Horton. It may be obvious that Chelsea House, doing a number of books a year by the same author, thought it a prudent marketing strategy to give the author more than one name. Horton's Western stories are concerned most of all with character, and it is the characters that drive the plots rather than the other way around. It is unfortunate he died at such a relatively early age. Many of his novels, after Street & Smith abandoned Chelsea House, were published only in British editions, and Robert J. Horton was never to appear at all in paperback books. *Riders of Paradise* will be his next **Five Star Western**.